LOVE ON THE ROCKS?

"I just found out that I need to go out of town," Jonathan said. "I'll be gone almost a whole week. It's a management training program."

"Congratulations, honey! That's great," Stephanie said. "Does this mean you'll get a promotion soon?"

"Probably. But things were sort of rocky between us this week, and I don't want you to think I'm doing this on purpose," Jonathan said.

"I wouldn't think that," Stephanie said. "It's your job. Anyway, maybe spending some time apart will be good for us."

NANCY DREW ON CAMPUS™

Available from ARCHWAY Paperbacks

Nancy Drew on Campus™ #24

In the Spotlight

Carolyn Keene

AN ARCHWAY PAPERBACK
Published by POCKET BOOKS
New York London Toronto Sydney Tokyo Singapore

AN ARCHWAY PAPERBACK *Original*

An Archway Paperback published by
POCKET BOOKS, a division of Simon & Schuster Inc.
1230 Avenue of the Americas, New York, NY 10020

ISBN: 0-671-00216-3

First Archway Paperback printing November 1997

10 9 8 7 6 5 4 3 2 1

CHAPTER 1

What do you think is the best food to eat on a date?" Montana Smith asked, staring at the bowl of soup in front of her. It was supposed to be minestrone, but at Wilder's laid-back campus dive, the Cave, it could be anything.

"You mean the easiest thing to eat?" Nikki Bennett asked. "The thing that is the least messy and won't fall off your fork the way this tabbouleh salad keeps doing?" She demonstrated her point by lifting a forkful to her mouth and losing half of it on the way.

"No, not the easiest thing to eat. The food that will put you, you know, in the most romantic mood," Montana said. She leaned back in her chair, taking a sip of iced tea. Her long blond curls fell over the back of the chair.

1

Kara Verbeck put down her grilled cheese and tomato sandwich. "Why do you want to know, Montana? Are you planning something we should know about?"

"This wouldn't have anything to do with a certain singer in a certain band with a certain way of making you swoon whenever he walks by, would it?" Nikki asked. Teasing Montana about Ray Johansson, lead singer of the band Radical Moves, was a favorite game of Montana's friends.

"Don't I wish!" Montana said. "No, it's for our radio show. I'm trying to think of some outrageous ideas for call-in topics. And nothing gets people's attention faster than love and food."

"Well, nothing gets my attention faster, that's for sure," Kara joked.

"Speaking of love . . ." Nikki nodded toward the entrance.

Ray Johansson was walking into the Cave with a stack of posters cradled under one arm. He was wearing a broken-in black leather jacket and faded blue jeans that were torn at the knees. His thick black hair was artfully windblown.

Montana felt a rush when Ray looked over at her and smiled. His face alone was enough to make her weak, and his beautiful, deep voice always took her breath away.

"Ray, what are you doing here?" Montana asked as he approached their table.

Ray held up the stack of posters. "I'm on poster duty."

Montana skimmed the announcement. "Cool!

2

You guys are playing at Club Z tomorrow night. That's great."

"Yeah, we're psyched," Ray said. "We haven't played at Jason's club for a while. Not to mention the fact that we could really use the money."

"Why don't you have a seat and hang out with us? I could buy you a sandwich, seeing as you're a penniless, starving musician," she offered.

"Thanks, Montana, but I need to put up the rest of these posters," Ray said.

"Can I help?" Montana asked. "We could get the work done in half the time. Then maybe we could go out for coffee, or—"

"I've got a rehearsal as soon as I'm done," Ray said, putting one of the larger posters on the Cave's bulletin board. "Thanks, anyway. See you guys tomorrow night at the show." Ray waved to their table, then strode out of the Cave.

"See you *guys* at the show?" Montana wailed. "What kind of a goodbye is that?"

"A casual one?" Kara suggested.

"Way casual," Nikki added.

Montana shook her head. "Is the guy dense, or does he just not like me?"

"Definitely dense," Nikki said. "How could he not be interested in you? You two have always gotten along."

"Yeah, only he treats me like I'm his little sister or something," Montana said. She didn't know how much longer she could stand this. She was totally attracted to Ray and had tried a dozen times to let him know, but he always shied away from her. "Is

3

he afraid of getting hurt? Does he just not want to be with anyone right now—or is it me?" she wondered out loud, staring at the Radical Moves poster.

"He was involved with Ginny for kind of a long time," Kara said. "Maybe he's still getting over her."

"Or maybe he's just oblivious to the way you feel," Nikki added.

"What do you think I should do about it?" Montana asked.

"You don't feel comfortable asking him out and *telling* him how you feel?" suggested Kara.

"No way!" Montana held up a hand as if to protect herself from the mere thought of it.

"Keep trying, then, I guess," Nikki said. "Eventually he'll realize that you're the right one for him."

"Unless he's crazy. In which case you don't want to go out with him anyway," Kara pointed out.

Montana laughed. "What would I do without you guys?"

"Be really, really, really confused about your love life," Kara said. "Now eat your soup before it gets cold."

"Okay, Mom."

"Our show's going to be a total hit," said Michael Gianelli, Nancy Drew's cohost for *Headlines,* the new student TV show. Michael and Nancy sat with Professor Stanley Trenton in his office, planning the premiere lead story. "It'll be a major success. After all, *I'll* be in front of the camera, won't I?"

Nancy fought the urge to say that she hoped that wouldn't ruin their chances of appealing to the audience altogether. Not that Michael wasn't appealing. Physically, anyway. He was tall and had short dark hair and penetrating deep brown eyes with long lashes. Only his personality left a little to be desired, like humility, compassion, basic courtesy. From what Nancy could tell so far, he was an amazing flirt. Not to mention an immense pain to work with every day.

"Charismatic personalities aside, what story is going to make your first show such a hit?" Professor Trenton asked.

"The tuition hike," Nancy said, glad to get down to business. "Our goal is to deal with issues that affect students most. Not only will the hike have a huge impact on individual lives, it'll alter the character of the university in the long run by limiting access to only those who can afford the higher costs. We'll interview students from different levels of income to find out how they plan to deal with the additional financial burden and then see what the president of the university has to say in response."

Professor Trenton nodded. "Good instinct," he said. "That's not the story I chose for your first show, but it's definitely an important issue. And your approach is sound."

"I disagree," Michael said.

"Excuse me?" Nancy asked.

"No, excuse *me,*" Professor Trenton said, leaning back in his chair. "I thought I was the professor around here."

"You are, of course," Michael said. "I just think that the tuition story will have to be done the right way to be appealing. Since it's our first show, we want to make sure we really grab the audience."

"What are you suggesting?" Nancy asked. "We run a lottery and hand out scholarships on our first show?" She'd seen several local news stations use contests and prizes to increase their viewership.

"Hear me out," Michael suggested. "I was thinking along the lines of grabbing them with sensational, shocking news."

"Sensational, shocking news generally spells trash," Nancy commented.

"You want to hear my idea before passing judgment?" Michael didn't wait for an answer. "Instead of looking at the raise in tuition from a traditional viewpoint, we go at it more aggressively. We explore whether students are really getting what they're paying for. We check out professors' salaries, investigate who has tenure. Who deserves it, and who doesn't. With higher education becoming more and more expensive, I think we have to evaluate whether the education we're getting here is worth the cost."

Nancy hated to admit it, but Michael's approach did have some merit. A cost-benefit analysis was worthwhile, although she didn't think it was so sensational or shocking. "That wouldn't be a bad way to cover *my* story," she said, "but it would take an incredible amount of research into Wilder's finances, books—"

"If you could get anyone to cooperate with you over at the Wilder registrar and accounting offices," Professor Trenton added.

"Hey, isn't that what journalism's all about? Being so aggressive that sources *have* to cooperate with you?" Michael offered.

"According to some people, yes," Nancy shot back. "Others would call that obnoxious."

Michael grinned at her. "Hey, whatever it takes, Nance."

Nancy glared at him. *"Don't* call me Nance. Okay?" He didn't know her well enough to use a nickname. "Unless you want to be called Mike. Or is it Mikey?"

"Lighten up! I get your point, *Nancy,"* Michael replied, shaking his head. "Some people are so sensitive."

"And some people are very insensitive," Nancy said, growing angrier by the second. "And arrogant and self-centered—"

Professor Trenton cleared his throat. "Make sure you two work out any personal differences *off* the air, all right? Now, I'd like to tell you about my idea for the first show." He pulled a scrap of paper off the bulletin board behind his desk. "Here it is in a nutshell: successful student entrepreneurs." He glanced at Nancy and Michael, who both looked a little less than enthusiastic. "Not sensational enough for you, eh? Well, it's a good, solid start, and I think you should consider it—*seriously."*

Before Michael had a chance to open his big mouth and say what he honestly thought of the professor's idea, Nancy charged ahead.

"Sounds great, really," Nancy said. "In fact, I know a couple of student entrepreneurs we could start with. One of my suitemates started her own computer consulting business with a friend," Nancy said. "And another friend of mine, Jason Lehman, is the owner of Club Z. He's out of school, but only just." Jason's brother, Emmet, dated one of Nancy's suitemates.

"*You* know the owner of Club Z?" Michael asked pointedly.

"Yes. Why are you so surprised?" Nancy asked.

"Well, it's just that you didn't strike me as the club type," Michael said.

"And what's that supposed to mean?" Nancy said.

"Nothing." Michael shrugged. "I just thought you were the stay-at-home-and-study-on-a-Friday-night type."

"That just shows again that you don't know anything about me, and you should quit making assumptions," Nancy said.

"Okay, okay. Time out," Professor Trenton said. "We have a show to put together."

Michael and Nancy sat glaring at each other.

"If you two can't get along for more than a couple of minutes, *Headlines* won't succeed. So, listen up. Your personal problems get put aside. You learn to cooperate." Professor Trenton softened his tone a little. "You don't have to become friends, but you do need to become effective coworkers."

Nancy nodded. "I understand."

"Hey, I can work with anyone," Michael said.

Nancy groaned inwardly. Maybe he could work with anyone, but faced with Michael Gianelli, she wasn't sure she could say the same.

"I can't believe opening night is three days from now," Brian Daglian said. "I'm psyched, aren't you?"

"I'm psyched, but I'm also completely wiped out." Bess Marvin sat down beside Brian on the stage. She had just returned from changing out of her costume after the first dress rehearsal for *Cat on a Hot Tin Roof.*

Bess had won the lead role of Maggie in the play and Brian was her leading man, Brick, an alcoholic ex-football player. Their characters were trapped in a bad marriage. Since Brian and Bess were super-close friends, they had a lot of fun goofing around, pretending to be a couple.

"I'm glad we're finally about to stage this thing," Bess said with an exhausted smile. "I don't know how much longer I could deal with this rehearsal schedule."

"I'll be happy to fill in," Daphne Gillman offered in a snide tone. "If the work's too much for you, Bess."

Daphne, who felt she deserved the lead in every Wilder production, had also auditioned for the role of Maggie. She deeply resented Bess for getting cast, especially since Bess was a freshman. Unfortunately for Bess, Daphne was the understudy for Maggie, which meant they had to spend a lot of time together in rehearsals and meetings. It also meant that Bess was constantly subjected to Daphne's stream of insults and complaints.

"Bess has a ton of energy," Brian said, standing up to Daphne. "And even if she were dying of consumption, she'd make a better Maggie than you."

Daphne glared at him. "I was *talking* to Bess."

"Go ahead," Brian said. "Talk. Just leave out the insults and innuendos."

"I didn't mean to insult you," Daphne said, turning to Bess. "But if you do feel sort of run-down, I can understand. What with your eating problem and all . . ."

Bess was stunned. How did Daphne know about her bulimia? No one knew except her closest friends—and her roommate, Leslie King. "Where did you hear about that?" Bess spat the question at Daphne.

"Bess," Daphne said, syrupy sweet. "I care about you. I pay attention to what's going on in your life."

"Meaning you're a gossip hound," Brian said.

"You," Daphne said, pointing at Brian, "stay out of this conversation."

"Stop!" Bess cried. "I don't care what you heard. It's none of your business. I am just fine, so stop paying attention to my life."

Daphne gave her a cool, calculating look. "Bess,

I only want what's best for the play. I don't want to let the audience down."

"And *Bess* won't disappoint the audience," Brian told her. "So quit worrying, if that's what you call it."

"Fine." Daphne swept her scarf around her neck. "See you guys at rehearsal tomorrow." She left with a flourish, as if she were making a grand exit off the stage.

Brian walked after her, imitating her strut. "Fine!"

Bess cracked up. "You have this incredible way of making me laugh just when things are getting rotten. You know that, don't you?"

"I love making you laugh," Brian said. "Especially after all that serious stuff in the play, about how I hate you and everything."

"Almost as much as I hate you." Bess gave him one of what Jeanne Glasseburg, the director, called her "angry Maggie" looks.

"Hey, some of us are going over to the Student Union. Want to come?" Brian asked, putting a hand on Bess's shoulder.

"That depends," Bess said under her breath. "Is Daphne going?"

Brian laughed. "Hel-*lo*-o! I don't *think* so."

"Then I'll meet you guys there in a half hour or so. Jeanne wants to work on some technical stuff with Mr. Light, Mr. Sound, and Ms. Star."

"Maybe you are a bit overworked, Bess. What are you talking about."

"You know. Justin Beckett, the lighting director?

Max Ridgefield the sound man? And, me, the star?"

Brian put on his mortician's face and patted her shoulder sympathetically.

"How come I'm never as funny as you, Brian?" Bess asked half seriously.

Brian broke up laughing. "Oh, no. I've created a monster. And to think I had to convince *you* to audition for anything."

Bess laughed. "See you at the Union. Save me a seat, okay?"

Half an hour later Bess headed out the back door of the Hewlitt Center for the Performing Arts.

She wondered for a second whether she should be going to the Student Union after all. What if everyone there was pigging out? She might not be able to resist. It might set off her eating disorder.

As Bess turned the corner of the building, deep in thought, a dark figure leaped out in front of her. Before she could register what was happening, Bess heard a hissing sound and suddenly her eyes seemed to be on fire.

CHAPTER 2

Bess screamed, her eyes burning. She couldn't see a thing, and her throat felt as if it were closing up. She could barely breathe. Gasping for air, she staggered blindly on the sidewalk.

"Oh! Oh, no!" Bess heard a voice cry out in front of her. Behind her, she heard the theater door fly open and footsteps run down the stairs.

Justin and Max ran to her rescue.

"Bess! Daphne! What happened?" Max shouted.

"Bess, are you okay?" Justin took her arm and guided her to the back steps of the building.

Bess sat down, rubbing her eyes with the sleeve of her jacket. "My eyes are burning, my nose, my throat . . ."

"It's all my fault. Bess, I'm *so* sorry," Daphne said.

"What did you do to her?" Justin demanded.

"It's just a little pepper spray," Daphne explained.

"Pepper spray? Are you crazy?" Justin shouted. He turned to Bess. "Let's go inside where it's warmer. I'll get some water to rinse your eyes out. I'll be right back."

"It'll be all right, Bess," Max said, sitting beside her and gently rubbing her back for comfort. "The effects don't last that long."

"Daphne? That was *you?*" Bess sputtered between miserable moans.

"I was coming back to get my notebook for French class. I left it backstage."

"That doesn't explain why you attacked Bess," Max said.

"I didn't know it was her! I heard a noise, and I got scared," Daphne said. "I always carry pepper spray with me after dark."

Justin came out of Hewlitt, carrying a cup of water. He splashed some of it on Bess's face to bathe her eyes. "How could you do this?" he demanded of Daphne. "Bess is in serious pain here!"

"Look, I said I was sorry," Daphne said in an irritated tone. "I was looking after my own safety. Wilder isn't crime-free, you know. Stuff happens. As a woman, especially, I need to defend myself."

Bess frowned. The pain in her eyes was beginning to lessen. From what she could tell, anyone who came near Daphne needed protection, not the other way around. "You could have asked who I was first," Bess complained.

"Bess is right," Justin added. "You were way out of line, Daphne."

"I was only trying to look out for myself," Daphne repeated with a dramatic sulk.

"How unusual," Bess muttered.

Daphne slung her backpack over her shoulder. "What was that, Bess?"

"Nothing," Bess said bitterly.

"Bess, I feel so awful. I don't know what I'd do if I harmed you."

Probably celebrate, Bess thought as she doused her eyes with water again.

"I mean, if you couldn't perform this Friday, I'd feel terrible," Daphne went on.

"Daphne, save your acting for the theater, okay?" Bess snapped.

"My acting? What do you mean?" Daphne put a hand to her throat.

"You're acting like you care about me," Bess said angrily. "We all know you'd like nothing better than for me to drop out of this play, so you could take my place."

"I didn't say that," Daphne protested.

"You've been suggesting it ever since I got the part," Bess said, getting to her feet. "Well, you can forget about it. Opening night is Friday, and I'll be there."

"Bess, can I walk you somewhere?" Justin offered, standing up beside her.

"Thanks, Justin," Bess said. "I could use the help."

"Oh, it's no problem," Justin said with a smile. "I'll take you wherever you need to go."

"Thanks. You, too, Max. Thanks for coming to my rescue." Bess tried to smile.

"You're welcome," Max replied. "You okay, now?"

"Come on, Bess." Justin took Bess's arm and held her tightly against his side as they headed off toward the Student Union.

"So, what's for dinner tonight?" Stephanie Baur asked her husband Tuesday evening, as they both wrapped up their shifts at Berrigan's Department Store.

"Hmm, will it be spaghetti? Fettuccine? Or bow-tie pasta?" Jonathan Baur replied with a teasing smile. He reached out and gently tugged Stephanie's long brown hair.

Stephanie groaned. "Do we have to eat at home, again?" She felt as if she'd eaten more pasta in the last few weeks than the entire population of Italy had.

Ever since Stephanie's father had cut off her money supply, she'd had to watch every penny. That was how she'd ended up working at Berrigan's and meeting Jonathan, who was a floor manager there. Stephanie tried to pretend that being a poor young couple was romantic, but she didn't know if she could stomach yet another night of watching TV and staring into a steaming bowl of noodles.

"Honey, if we skimp during the week . . ." Jonathan began.

"I know, we can go out on the weekend." Stephanie finished his familiar excuse. "But it's only Tuesday. I don't know if I can wait that long."

"Hey, I'm glad it's Tuesday. Some of our favorite TV shows are on tonight," Jonathan said. Stephanie couldn't tell if he was serious or not. "Come on, Steph," he continued. "We'll have a quiet dinner together, you can get some homework done, we'll snuggle on the couch . . ."

"I guess that sounds okay," Stephanie agreed.

"Okay? Is that all?" Jonathan asked, squeezing her hand more tightly.

"It sounds wonderful," Stephanie said, smiling at him. "Will you wait for me? I need to grab my bag from the employees lounge."

"Will I wait for you?" Jonathan leaned over and kissed her lightly on the lips. "Stephanie, I'm married to you. I promised to wait for you, in sickness and in health, in hours of shopping and trying on clothes—"

"Yeah, yeah. Very funny," Stephanie said, playfully hitting his arm. "Hold on, I'll be right back." She left the sales floor and headed to the employee lounge.

She knew Jonathan was trying really hard to make their marriage a success, to make her happy, but it just didn't seem real to her yet. Something was missing. And Stephanie had recently figured out what it was. A baby, she had decided, would solve all their problems.

The real problem was convincing Jonathan that they were ready to have a family. He was so practical, he'd probably have a million arguments against it. They should be more settled first or have more money or Stephanie should graduate from Wilder first. Stephanie felt ready for motherhood—no matter what Jonathan or anyone else thought. If a baby wouldn't make her feel committed to her marriage, what would?

"Oh, hi, Jackie. How's it going?" Stephanie asked, walking into the employee lounge.

Jackie Lanford turned around from her locker. "Hey, Stephanie, what are you up to?"

"Heading home," Stephanie said. "You, too?"

Jackie nodded. She glanced at the small address book in her hand. "Actually, I have to make some phone calls. I found out today that my regular baby-sitter has strep throat, and I've got to attend that buyers' seminar in Boston on Thursday and Friday." Jackie's words started tumbling out faster and faster. "There's no way I can take Molly all the way to Boston and put her in some strange day care center—"

"Jackie, relax," Stephanie said, putting a hand on her arm. Although Jackie was a single mom, she never seemed to stress out about it. If she was this upset, she needed help. "I can take care of Molly while you're gone," Stephanie volunteered.

"You? But what about school and work and—"

"No problem," Stephanie assured her. "It's only two days, right?"

"Well, yeah, but it's a lot of work," Jackie told her. "Are you sure?"

"Defintely," Stephanie said. "My schedule's really

light on those days." Was this perfect or what? Now she'd have a chance to test out motherhood before committing herself. She smiled at Jackie. "I'd love to take care of Molly."

"Stephanie, that would be great, but . . . well, I hate to ask you this—you're so nice to volunteer—but do you have any experience caring for a six-month-old infant?" Jackie said. "You don't exactly strike me as the baby-sitter type."

"Oh, sure." Stephanie decided not to be offended by Jackie's comment. "I have tons of experience," she lied.

"You do?" Jackie asked.

"I used to look after my twin baby cousins all the time," Stephanie said. Of course, her cousins had their own full-time nanny, but Stephanie had watched her take care of the twins. She wasn't a complete ignoramus when it came to babies. "I know how to change a diaper, if that's what you're asking. And Jonathan will be a big help."

"Fantastic. In that case, I'll gladly take you up on your offer," Jackie said.

"I won't let you down, Jackie," Stephanie promised.

Stephanie couldn't wait to tell Jonathan. Then again, she thought as she opened her locker, maybe she'd wait. If he didn't like the idea, she'd have to tell Jackie she couldn't do it. That would be mortifying. Besides, Jonathan wouldn't mind helping out. It would be like having a baby of their own.

* * *

"I wouldn't worry about Daphne," Brian said as they stopped outside Jamison Hall. Brian had walked Bess home from the Student Union. He wanted to make sure she was all right after her run-in with Daphne. "Seriously, I don't think she'd ever do anything to hurt you."

"She already has. *You* didn't get a blast of pepper spray in the face," Bess said, getting out her keys.

"True." Brian smiled apologetically. "I've heard that stuff really hurts."

"It's the worst," Bess said. "I felt as if I was on fire."

"I'm so sorry." Brian paused. "But I really don't think it was a plot." Bess raised an eyebrow. *"Really,"* Brian insisted.

"So you say. But if I get up to my room and find out it's been booby-trapped, Daphne will be number one on my list of suspects." Bess shook her head. "What *was* that girl thinking?"

"That's just it. I don't think she was," Brian said. "She couldn't have planned that. I mean, Daphne isn't exactly known for her incredible intelligence."

Bess laughed. "So she's actually too dumb to knock me out of the play?"

"Exactly." Brian leaned forward and gave Bess a hug.

"Thanks for walking me home," Bess told him, squeezing Brian tightly.

"No problem. See you tomorrow!" Brian started jogging across the campus quad toward his own dorm.

Bess slipped into the dorm, closing the door firmly behind her. What would she do without Brian's friendship? He was her main support. He'd helped her prepare for auditions and was constantly telling her how good she was. He understood her struggle with bulimia, while even Nancy and George didn't truly get it. He had held her hand at the Student Union as she obsessed about all the greasy, high-calorie, mouth-watering food everyone else was eating.

As Bess headed for the stairs, she paused by the vending machine in the dorm lobby. The glass front seemed to sparkle at her. Why was this so hard? Just keep going, she commanded herself. Move, legs, move!

But instead, she stood staring at the packages of M&M's, as if they were the last thing on earth to eat. She'd been so responsible at the Union earlier, with her diet soda and a small bag of pretzels. Couldn't she have just a few M&M's? She could promise herself she'd eat only the green ones. Didn't she deserve a reward after the hard day— not to mention night—she'd had? After all, no one could expect her to be perfect twenty-four hours a day.

Bess rummaged in her pocket for some change. Good thing she'd saved all those quarters for laundry. She jammed a couple into the vending machine and pressed the button for the M&M's. The package made a delicious small *kthunk* sound as it landed in the bin. She reached in and pulled it out. It felt very small in her hand. That'll never be enough, Bess thought. She fed several more quarters into the machine. Before she stopped, she had four packages of M&M's stuffed into the outside pocket of her backpack. She couldn't even zip the pocket shut.

She stared at the bags of candy. Did she really want to do this? It would be a giant step backward. Bess knew the routine: She'd eat the candy and then start feeling guilty. She'd make herself sick, so she wouldn't gain any weight. Then it would almost seem as if she hadn't given in at all. Almost, but not quite. She'd start to feel even guiltier than before and then she'd eat more to feel better, and it would start all over again. And over, and over—until she found herself feeling as desperate as she had two weeks ago.

I have to be strong, Bess told herself. I have to beat this!

She dumped the M&M's into a trash can, then ran upstairs to her room. She had to talk with Vicky, her therapist, right away before she decided to run back downstairs and retrieve the candy.

She jiggled open the door with her key. Her roommate, Leslie, wasn't home. Probably at the library studying, Bess figured. She picked up the telephone and punched in Vicky's home number. The phone rang four times, and then an answering machine picked up.

Disappointed, Bess sighed as she dropped her backpack on the floor. "Hi, Vicky," she began. "It's Bess. I'm sorry to bother you, but you said call anytime, and—"

"Bess?" Vicky came on the line. "Hi! Sorry, I just walked in the door."

"Oh. Well, are you sure I'm not bothering you? I didn't realize how late it was," Bess said, glancing at her alarm clock. It was nearly eleven o'clock. "I just got home, and I really needed to talk—"

"It's okay, Bess. I wouldn't have told you to call anytime if I didn't mean it," Vicky said. "So, what's up?"

"This is so embarrassing," Bess began.

"Bess, nothing's that embarrassing," Vicky assured her. "We know each other too well by now for you to hold back."

"You're right." Bess smiled. "We have been through a lot. Okay, here's what happened. I'm okay now, but after our dress rehearsal tonight, this girl Daphne—my understudy, who's constantly giving me a hard time—sprayed me with pepper spray. She said it was a mistake, but she's been trying to take over my part in the play ever since I got it," Bess explained.

"Oh, how awful, Bess. Do you think she decided to attack you?" Vicky asked.

"I'm not sure. She loves making me feel bad, though," Bess said. "She does everything she can to remind me of what a rough time I've had lately. Tonight she even brought up my bulimia—in front of other people! I don't even know how she knew about it."

"Sounds like she's decided to take out her own anger and frustration on you. I'm sorry, Bess." Vicky paused and Bess felt tears come to her eyes.

"How did you deal with the attack, Bess? Was Brian there?"

"I met him and a bunch of other cast members at the Student Union after rehearsal. I thought I'd take your advice and socialize more," Bess said.

"And how did it go?" Vicky asked.

"It went okay, I guess. Brian and I talked a lot. But then when I got home, I felt like . . . like I'd been cheated or something. Like I wasn't in control without a friend around to watch me. And after the attack and all, I wanted comfort," Bess explained. "So there I was, face-to-face with the candy machine in the lobby—"

"No, anything but that," Vicky said. She had once told Bess that vending machines had been her personal enemies when she was going through her own eating problems in college. "Why do they put those things in dorms, anyway? So what happened?"

"I broke down and bought some M&M's," Bess said. "Then I realized I didn't really want them and I threw them out. But I still kind of feel like running back downstairs and picking them out of the trash."

"Can you tell me why you'd do that?" Vicky asked. "Maybe once you realize what your motivation is, you won't want to act on it."

Bess started telling Vicky about her feelings that night, and the intense scrutiny she felt she was under when she was onstage. As she talked, she realized that she had calmed herself down.

But what would I have done if Victoria hadn't

walked in the door just then and picked up the phone? Bess wondered.

Nancy checked the end of the book she'd been assigned to read for her Western Civ class and discovered she had forty more pages to go.

She glanced sleepily at the clock on the wall of the lounge. She had an hour and a half to shower and get dressed before she was supposed to meet Michael. They'd planned to work out a schedule for interviews and studio editing time over breakfast.

Reva Ross's door opened, and the tall, thin girl walked out into the lounge neatly dressed in cigarette pants and a cashmere sweater. "What are you doing?" she asked Nancy, running a comb through her dark brown hair. "Studying already?"

"I've got a ton of work, as usual," Nancy said. "You?"

"Of course. But shouldn't you be getting dressed?" Reva asked.

"Eventually. You're looking good for this hour. Got a date?" Nancy teased.

"Well, I want to look good for my television debut," Reva said with a laugh. "But aren't you going to be there this morning when Michael Gianelli interviews us for *Headlines?* I thought you two were the cohosts."

"What are you talking about?" Nancy asked. "I don't know anything about an interview. I mean, I mentioned to him that we *should* interview you, but we didn't make any definite plans."

"Didn't Michael tell you? We set up this interview last night, for first thing this morning," Reva said. "Eight o'clock."

"You're kidding," Nancy cried. "What a jerk!"

"Did I miss something?" Reva asked.

"He's supposed to meet me for breakfast at nine. He never mentioned interviewing you first," Nancy explained. "Which means he wanted to scoop the story and take all the credit for himself, even though I'm the one who knows you."

Reva raised her eyebrows. "You get along really well with this guy, don't you?"

"We're like this." Nancy held up a finger on each hand and moved them as far apart as she could. "Where's the interview going to be?"

"At the computer lab," Reva said. "Michael said it would make a good backdrop, and since we get a lot of our clients from there, it makes sense. Anyway, I'd better get going. Hey, Nancy, why don't you just come with me?"

Nancy grinned. "Good idea."

Nancy got ready as fast as she could. She put on the first clothes she grabbed, washed her face, and ran a comb through her hair.

All the while, she stewed over the situation. If Michael thought he could steal an interview right from under her nose, he was wrong. And he was just about to find out how wrong!

CHAPTER 3

There he is. What a weasel," Nancy complained to Reva as they walked up to the computer center. Michael was taking the studio video camera out of the backseat of a small blue sports car. So far, he was totally oblivious to their presence.

He was wearing a crisp white button-down shirt and tie, with blue jeans. He seemed casually professional—the look they'd agreed on for the show—and extremely handsome, considering it was only eight in the morning. But who cared about his appearance when he acted like such a creep?

Michael walked around to the driver's side of the car, the video camera propped nonchalantly on his shoulder. Nancy could see that a woman with long blond hair was driving the car—in her pajamas!

Okay, Nancy thought, so maybe she wasn't doing

much better, in an old sweatshirt and jeans, but she hadn't had time to put together an outfit. At least she was *dressed.*

"Thanks for the ride. I still can't believe I slept through the alarm," Michael said.

"I can," the woman replied.

Michael leaned in the open window and kissed her. "I'll see you, okay?"

"Definitely," she replied. " 'Bye, Mikey."

I may be sick, Nancy thought.

Michael turned around to head into the building and nearly crashed into Nancy and Reva, who were standing on the sidewalk.

"Nancy!" he exclaimed. "What are you doing here? And you must be Reva. I'm Michael. It's a pleasure to meet you." He grinned, reaching out to shake Reva's hand. "Is Andy already inside?"

"I'm not sure. We just got here," Reva said.

"Oh. Well, in that case, let's go inside and get started," Michael said.

"Not so fast." Nancy held up a hand just as Michael stepped forward. He walked right into it, and she pressed her hand firmly against his chest.

He glanced down at her hand. "Well, this is interesting."

Nancy felt herself begin to blush. She quickly took her hand away. "Why didn't you tell me about this interview?"

"I think I'll go inside and make sure the place looks decent," Reva said nervously. "Meet you guys at the computer lab."

* * *

"Well?" Nancy prompted. "I'm waiting."

"Nancy, are you mad at me?" Michael asked in a tone of innocent disbelief. "I don't understand why."

"Because we're supposed to be doing this story together. And the first chance you get, *you* pursue *my* leads for an interview," Nancy stated flatly. "Is that what you consider working together?"

"Look, I was going to tell you about it at breakfast," Michael began.

"And what good would that have done? The interview would have been over," Nancy said. "Do you have some burning need to be the only guy on camera? Is that it? You don't want to share the spotlight?"

"Relax, Nance."

Nancy raised her eyebrows, looking as if she might haul off and hit him.

"*Nancy.* Sorry." He apologized quickly. "It's not like that at all. See, all I'd planned to do was set up a few interviews for us. But when I contacted Andy last night, he said that he was going to be out of town for a few days. I just thought we'd better shoot the interview this morning." At least the part about Andy leaving town was the truth.

"You mean you thought *you'd* better shoot the interview," Nancy pointed out.

"Now—" Michael began to protest.

"Couldn't you have called me to tell me about it?" Nancy asked. "Or asked Reva to tell me? You know we live in the same suite."

"I guess I was too wrapped up in making all the

29

arrangements. Anyway, I didn't know if you'd have time," Michael said. "Apparently you do." He glanced at Nancy's clothes. He couldn't believe how great she looked, in spite of her worn, paint-splattered sweatshirt and faded old jeans. Did she wake up that gorgeous?

"Of course I'd have time," Nancy said. *"Head-lines* is my number one priority these days. I'd *find* the time."

"Okay, okay . . . but I don't know if you're quite ready to go on camera in that outfit." Michael reached out to finger the torn, ratty sleeve of Nancy's faded River Heights High sweatshirt. "It really doesn't do you justice."

Nancy glared at him. "So I'll operate the camera," she said. "Come on, let's go."

"Whatever you say. You're the boss." Michael grinned at Nancy.

"No one's the boss. Don't you get it?" Nancy shook her head and walked into the building.

All I get, Michael thought as he followed her, *is that I've got to be working with the most demanding woman in the world!*

Montana knocked lightly on the door to the loft that Radical Moves rented as rehearsal space. "Hello? Anyone home?" she called.

"Come on in!" a deep voice replied.

Montana gently pushed the door open. "Hi. Sorry to interrupt."

"You're not interrupting anything," Cory Mc-Dermott, the band's lead guitarist, told her. "We're taking a break. Well, I guess that much is obvious." He lay down on the ratty green-and-yellow plaid couch. All of the furniture in the loft had been picked up secondhand—some of it straight off the street.

"Yeah, it's a little quiet around here compared to usual." Montana smiled at Ray, who was straddling a dilapidated wood chair, his arms hanging over its back. "So, how's it going? Ready for the gig at Club Z tonight?"

Ray shrugged. "I think so."

"Come on, man. You've got to get more psyched than that," Cory said. "Have some coffee or something."

Montana smacked her forehead with the palm of her hand. "I knew I forgot something. I was going to bring you guys a thermos of espresso."

"That's okay. You don't need to worry about us," Cory said.

"No—maybe not," Montana said. "But bringing gifts usually helps when you want to ask someone a favor." She looked anxiously at Ray.

"Ask away," he prompted.

Don't tempt me! Montana thought. "I wanted to know if you'd come on our radio show again. It was such a success last time. We had way more calls than we could handle, and—well, what do you say? Do you think you could come back on Saturday?" Montana looked at Ray as she finished her thoughts silently. *Then you could stay afterward and we could talk in private, maybe go out to dinner, catch a movie . . .*

Ray didn't say anything. Montana figured her ESP just wasn't getting through to him.

"Do you need all of us?" Karin Messer asked. "I'm afraid Austin and I can't make it." Karin was the band's female lead vocalist and Austin Rusche played drums.

"Whoever can make it. But, Ray, I have to say that you were kind of the showcase last time," Montana said. "You got a ton of calls, remember?"

"Why do girls always go after the lead singer?" Cory asked.

"You're just noticing that now?" Austin asked. "Dude, where have you been? I could move my drums to the front of the stage—and *still* no one would see me," Austin added.

"Okay, so, if I want to get noticed, I'll just have to act like that awful guitarist with Cybersound Hounds," Cory joked. He jumped off the couch, grabbed his guitar and slid across the floor on his knees, playing off-key and screaming. "That would get their attention." He smiled at Montana. "Too bad nobody would see that on the radio."

"Well, if you want a chance to stand out in front," Montana said, "maybe you should make sure to come with Ray to do the show."

"Fine with me. Yo, Johansson!" Cory shouted.

Ray looked at Cory and then Montana as if he hadn't been paying any attention during the last few minutes. "When did you say the interview was?"

"Saturday afternoon," Montana told him, feeling vaguely irritated. Here she was, offering him free publicity, and he could barely agree to come. Usually guys scrambled for Montana's attention. But not Ray. Maybe that's why I like him so much, she reflected.

"I can do it," Ray said. "Can you, Cory?"

"Where have you been, Ray? I'm already there," Cory told him. "Hey, thanks a lot, Montana. We really appreciate it," he added.

"You're welcome. I look forward to it," Montana said, smiling at them. "See you guys tonight at Club Z!"

She went out into the hallway and leaned against the wall. She had to do something about Ray. She had to let him know how she felt, and find out whether he cared. Tonight, she told herself. Tonight's the night.

"Thanks for meeting me here, you guys," Bess said, taking a seat in the cozy dining room of the Kappa house.

"No problem." George Fayne set down her plate, which was overflowing with an outrageously healthy salad. "I don't think I could stand another mystery meal at the dorm."

Nancy surveyed the bright room, decorated in a French country style.

"It's nice, Bess," Nancy said. "It's like having our own private cafeteria."

"Only students we *like* need apply," George said mischievously.

Bess smiled wryly. She was used to George's teasing her about the sorority. "But, we let you in, dear cousin," Bess tossed right back. Then she nodded in the direction of a table across the room where Soozie Beckerman sat. "And one or two others." Soozie had been a thorn in her side since before Bess had even pledged Kappa. Time to change the subject, Bess decided.

"So, what's been going on with you guys?"

"I've been busy dealing with Michael," Nancy said. "My cohost for *Headlines,* remember?"

Bess grinned. "You mean, do we remember the totally hot guy with dark brown hair and olive skin and the most—"

"Gigantic ego?" Nancy interrupted. "Yeah, that's him."

George laughed. "Sounds like things are going great."

"They were sort of tolerable until today," Nancy said heatedly. "He had the nerve to set up an interview with Reva and Andy for this morning without even telling me. He wanted all the credit for himself, not to mention the air time."

Nancy's anger surprised Bess. It wasn't like her.

"So *you'll* do an interview without him, and you'll be even," Bess suggested.

"But this isn't about getting even or getting credit. We're supposed to be working together," Nancy explained.

"At the risk of sounding like a Dear Angela column, let me say, it always takes time to get used to working with someone new," George said.

"That's true." Nancy took a spoonful of cottage cheese. "But I only have three and a half years of college left. I don't know if that's enough time—assuming I live through it. He's impossible."

"At least he's nice to look at," Bess said. "If someone's going to hog the air time, it might as well be somebody gorgeous."

"Traitor," Nancy muttered.

"Speaking of gorgeous men, how's everything with you and Will?" Bess asked George. Her cousin had been dating Will Blackfeather almost since they had arrived at Wilder.

"Fine, I guess." George shrugged. "We've both been really busy lately, and he's got to visit friends in Chicago this weekend. He told me to tell you he's sorry about missing your opening night."

"Well, as long as he shows up next weekend, I'll forgive him," Bess said.

"I'll pass that along," George promised.

"You must be crazed, Bess, what with opening night on Friday," Nancy commented. "How are the rehearsals going?"

"Great, except that after our rehearsal last night, I went outside and got pepper-sprayed," Bess told them.

"What?" George cried, almost dropping her fork. "Who did that?"

"Daphne Gillman," Bess said with distaste. "You know, the world's worst understudy? The one who hates my guts?"

"She hates you enough to attack you?" Nancy asked.

"Daphne said she didn't do it on purpose. She was coming back to Hewlitt to pick something up.

It was dark, and she heard me coming. She said she was acting in self-defense," Bess explained.

"She could have been," George said. "Ever since I was attacked outside the dorm, I'm much more apt to react to a strange noise. I carry pepper spray, too, you know."

"Remind me never to bump into you after dark then," Bess said. "Anyway, then I hung out with Brian at the Union for a while. I felt totally fine— well, almost—about not eating more than a small bag of pretzels. But when I got back to the dorm, I nearly went on a major binge."

"Why didn't you call me?" George said, putting her hand on Bess's arm.

"I called Vicky. We talked it out," Bess explained. "Thanks, but it's just not the same as talking to someone who's been through it."

"That's true for anything," Nancy agreed.

"Yeah. I was thinking about it this morning," Bess continued. "There must be other women on campus with the same problem. Not just women— men, too. And that's why I'm starting a support group for people with eating disorders."

George smiled. "Wow, Bess, that's a great idea."

"I can't believe there isn't one already," Nancy said. "I'd think a lot of people could use it."

"And you're just the person to lead it," George said.

"I'm not going to be in charge of anything," Bess said. "I'm just going to organize the first meeting. I made a few posters on the computer this morning, and I need you to help me decide which one I should use."

"Sure," Nancy said. "Let's see them."

Bess picked up her backpack and pulled out the three different posters she had designed.

"Bess, I'm really proud of you," George said.

"You have to be. I'm your cousin," Bess teased.

"No, I'm serious! Getting your life back on track, starring in a play, starting this group. It seems like all the pieces are coming together," George said.

Bess smiled, laying out the three posters on the table for them to look at. "Maybe they are, finally."

"You sure you want to lift that much?" Michael asked.

His best friend, Gus Lindgren, nodded with a competitive look in his eye.

"Okay. Whatever you say. I'll spot you." Michael stood over Gus, watching as he slowly lifted the barbells. "Easy . . . easy . . ." Gus pressed the weight over his head. "Excellent!" Michael said. He helped Gus set the weights back on their stand.

"Your turn," Gus said, standing up. "Of course, you might want to take off some of the weight first. You don't want to strain yourself."

"Oh, is that a challenge?" Michael brushed off his hands.

"Yes," Gus said.

"Then I accept, gladly. You know me. I love a challenge." Michael grinned and lay down on the padded bench.

"Speaking of challenges, what's up with you and

Lois Lane?" Gus asked as he spotted Michael's successful lift.

Michael laughed, setting the weights back down. "Who?"

"You know, your new coanchor. The one with the strawberry blond hair and the deep blue eyes. Remember?" Gus asked.

"Does she have blue eyes? Really?" Michael asked, standing up.

"Like you haven't noticed," Gus said, shaking his head.

"I haven't!" Michael protested.

"But you will," Gus said, settling back down on the bench for their next round of lifting. "In fact, I'd be willing to bet that you ask her out sometime in the next, oh, ten days, maybe?"

"Please. We work together," Michael said, sliding a heavier weight onto the end of the bar. "I'd never jeopardize that."

"Yeah, right," Gus said. "Tell that to Judy from your job in Maine last summer, or Kathryn from work-study freshman year, or Marilee—"

"Are you going to lift weights, or are you just going to lie there using up all the oxygen?" Michael asked. "I thought this was supposed to be a serious workout."

Michael was not in the mood to talk about Nancy. He hated to admit it, but he felt a tiny twinge of guilt for trying to scoop the interview that morning. But, hey, wasn't that part of the game of journalism? Getting the story first?

As for whether Nancy was pretty or not, that was hardly worth debating. She was beautiful. But Michael hadn't auditioned for *Headlines* to meet women. He'd done it for his future, for his career. If he happened to have a gorgeous coanchor, that was just one of the perks.

CHAPTER 4

I think I can; I think I can; I think I can," Bess mumbled as she walked up to the bulletin board at the Student Union. She was determined to put up her posters for the eating disorder support group even though she felt as if she were issuing a press release about her bulimia.

Bess carefully positioned the poster and was just about to shoot in the first staple when suddenly her book bag slipped off her shoulder. Her arm jerked to catch it and her posters went flying. She dropped the heavy staple gun on her foot. A half-dozen students came over to help her pick things up.

There and then, Bess decided to give up feeling embarrassed. She retrieved the stapler and put up her first poster with a flourish.

"Thanks, thanks, thanks," she said to everyone

helping her. "Fun and games with eating disorders," she said, pointing to the poster. "Everyone come, and bring a date." Her helpers laughed as they wandered off.

And you worry that you're not an actor? Bess asked herself.

Bess heard footsteps approach. Is someone already interested? She turned around and dropped the staple gun again, just missing her foot this time.

"Hi, Bess," Daphne said. She pointed toward the floor. "You dropped something."

Of all the people on campus to run into!

"Hi, Daphne." Bess tried to smile. She cringed as she bent down to pick up the staple gun, waiting to hear what Daphne would say next.

"How's it going?" Daphne asked. She gestured to the poster. "Not that good, huh?"

"Daphne, this"—Bess tapped her fingers on the poster—"*is* a good thing."

"Really." Daphne frowned. "Bess, I'm worried about you. Honestly."

"I bet you are," Bess grumbled.

"I am," Daphne insisted.

"Well, you can stop worrying," Bess told her. "I'm starting the support group so I can help other people."

"Do you really think you're up to that?" Daphne asked. "With the play opening and all."

"Look, Daphne. Spare me the false concern, okay? The way I see it, I need to be more worried about you and your pepper spray than me and my eating." Bess turned and walked out of the Union.

Her heart was pounding. She was beginning to understand why Daphne got under her skin the way she did: Daphne voiced Bess's own fear that she couldn't handle it all.

I'll just have to prove her wrong, Bess thought, walking determinedly to the library to put up more posters. "I think I can; I think I can; I think I can."

"Jason! Hey, this place looks great," Nancy said, striding into Club Z at eight o'clock Wednesday night. Jason had renovated an old warehouse into a large club with a brick interior. The building's exposed heating and water system pipes, ducts, and vents gave Club Z an urban, modern look. The club wouldn't open for another hour, which left her plenty of time for a quiet interview.

Michael came through the door behind her, carrying the video camera.

"You look pretty great yourself," Jason said, admiring Nancy's short red skirt and black top. "How are you doing?"

"Pretty good," Nancy said. "So, are you ready for your interview?"

"Definitely. But promise you'll go easy on me," Jason said. "And only shoot my good side. Wait a second. Which *is* my good side?"

Nancy laughed. "You'll look fine, don't worry."

Beside her, Michael cleared his throat loudly. "Ahem."

Nancy ignored him. "I thought we could do the interview at the bar. The black-and-white tiles will make a great background. Then we could pan around while you're talking, show the viewers what you've done with this old warehouse—"

"Ahem!" Michael said, a little more loudly this time. "Aren't you going to introduce me?"

"Oh. Right," Nancy said, turning around. "I knew I forgot something. This is Michael Gianelli. He's also working on *Headlines,*" she told Jason.

Michael stepped forward to shake Jason's hand. "Actually, we're cohosts," he said with an angry sideways glance at Nancy.

"Right," Nancy said with a phony smile. Two could play at this game. He had stolen their first interview, so she was going to make sure the second one was hers. "Anyway, Jason, I thought I could ask you a couple of questions now. Then we'll hang out and wait until the band starts playing, and shoot some footage of Club Z when it's rocking. How does that sound?"

"Great. I'll take all the free advertising I can get." Jason perched on a stool at the bar. "Okay, Nancy—shoot!"

"Michael, you don't mind running the camera, do you?" Nancy asked sweetly. "I've got a whole list of questions all ready for Jason, so I know what to ask."

"Uh-oh," Jason said, trying to peer at the sheet in Nancy's hand. "That looks worse than some exams I've taken."

"Don't worry. This is a piece of cake." She nodded toward Michael. "You can start recording now."

He was glaring at her. "Fine," he said coldly. "Whatever you say."

Nancy resisted the urge to pump her fist in victory. That would be tasteless gloating. She had just wanted to even the score, that was all.

"So," Michael began, stirring his ginger ale with a straw as they waited for things to liven up. "Nice interview. I guess that makes us even. You taped one interview and I taped one."

"Except that I was the one who thought of both interviews," Nancy said. "I had the contacts. Without me, you wouldn't have known where to begin."

"Please. I'm not helpless," Michael said with a dry laugh.

"Uh-huh. Not so helpless that you didn't need someone in pajamas to drive you to this morning's interview," Nancy said.

"For your information, she's just a friend," Michael said, acting a bit startled.

"Uh-huh."

"Hey, life goes on. At least *I* don't date someone whose idea of fashion is beat-up cowboy boots," Michael replied. "Not to mention being a lousy writer and reporter—"

"Are you talking about Jake Collins?" Nancy asked, dumbfounded. "You think he's a bad writer?"

Michael patted his mouth, pretending to yawn. "Bor-ing."

"You are so wrong," Nancy said. "And how do you know I was dating him?"

"I'm in the journalism department, in case you haven't noticed," Michael said. "Jake and I share some classes, and as any *good* reporter knows, if you keep your eyes open, you notice things."

"Well, apparently your eyes weren't open wide enough," Nancy said. "Or you'd know that Jake and I broke up a little while ago."

"Oh. Well, good for you," Michael said.

Nancy frowned. "Why is that good for me?"

"Because. The guy was all wrong for you," Michael said, shaking his head. He took a sip of ginger ale and leaned back in his chair, watching her.

True, Nancy thought, but what gave Michael the right to say so? He barely knew her, and he didn't seem to know Jake that well, either. "Oh, really," Nancy said, feeling her cheeks flush. "And I'm supposed to take this relationship advice from someone who hasn't gone out with one woman for more than—what? Two weeks, tops?"

"How do you know that?" Michael asked.

Nancy shrugged. "I can tell." She wondered whether any woman could stand being with Michael for more than two weeks.

Michael pointed his straw at her. "Just like I can tell that you've got lousy taste in men."

"And what's that supposed to mean?" Nancy asked with a superior laugh. "That I haven't asked you out yet?"

"Don't be silly. Of course that doesn't exactly *help* your record, but I won't hold it against you," Michael said, grinning slyly. "No, all I'm saying is that if you want to be happy, you'd better let me find a guy for you to date."

"Why would I need *your* help?"

"Because left on your own, you picked Jake Collins." Michael shook his head.

"Hey, there's nothing wrong with Jake, okay?" Nancy said.

"Wow. Loyal to your ex." Michael nodded in admiration. "Don't see that very often."

"See, this might be hard to understand. But some of us actually *care* about the people we date," Nancy said.

Michael laughed. "Maybe I just haven't found the right woman yet. Maybe I'll be incredibly committed when that happens."

"I wouldn't hold my breath," Nancy said. "It's hard to picture you being committed to anyone but yourself."

"Hey, that's a little harsh. Just because I haven't found the right woman doesn't mean I can't commit. Just like the fact that you can't find the right guy doesn't mean you're too high-maintenance for anyone to deal with." He smiled at her. "Some people might say that, but *I* wouldn't."

"Oh, no. Never," Nancy said. "Just like I'd never say that you've simply got lousy taste in women."

"Who knows? Maybe I do." Michael shrugged. "Maybe we both have bad taste. In that case, we should start choosing each other's dates—since we're so bad at choosing for ourselves."

"That's not a bad idea," Nancy mused. "Though

I can just picture you setting me up with a real jerk."

"I'd never do that," Michael protested.

Nancy looked at him for a second. Well, as long as he didn't set her up with himself, it might be worth a shot. He definitely knew a different crowd than she did. It would be fun to meet some new guys. "Then what are we talking about here?"

"I'll set you up with someone I know. A guy who'd be perfect for you," Michael said.

"And I'll find a great date for you," Nancy said. "Are you free Friday night? We can go to the opening of *Cat on a Hot Tin Roof.*"

"Friday night," Michael replied, standing up. "It's a date."

As she watched Michael walk around the club, videotaping the band's opening number, Nancy wondered, What am I getting myself into?

"Stephanie! What are you doing here?" Kara asked.

"Nice to see you, too," Stephanie replied, raising one eyebrow. "What is this, the Wednesday Night Pizza Party?" She set her empty gym bag on the floor of her old suite.

"Like you don't remember," Reva teased. "Amazing how you showed up just in time for a fresh, hot slice." She held the open box out to Stephanie.

"Stephanie probably followed the pizza delivery guy up from the parking lot," Liz Bader said with a laugh. "He *was* cute."

Stephanie sighed. "If you must know," she said in an irritated tone, "his name's Conrad." Then she grinned. "Just kidding. I came by to get some stuff I left when I moved over to Jonathan's."

"Oh. And we thought you were here to see us," Casey Fontaine, Stephanie's ex-roommate, said with a dejected pout.

"I am, I am!" Stephanie cried. "You guys are so sensitive." She wedged herself between Liz and Eileen on the couch and settled in. Then she reached for the cheesiest piece of pizza, carrying hot strings of mozzarella up to her mouth. "So what's new?"

"We're all going to Club Z tonight to hear Radical Moves play," Liz said.

"And to dance," Kara added.

"You're kidding," Stephanie said. "I'd love to see them again."

"So come with us." Casey said.

"I can't." Stephanie frowned. "I have to meet Jonathan for dinner when he gets off work at nine o'clock." She stared at the half-eaten slice of pizza in her hand. "Oops."

"Kind of late for dinner, isn't it?" Eileen asked.

"Yeah, but he's been working extra hours at the store, so we can save some money—" Stephanie stopped short. Get a hold of yourself, she thought. You sound pathetic! You can't go out, you don't have any money. . . . She couldn't let everyone think things were that bad. Even if they were, she'd hate for her old suitemates to know.

"Actually, we're saving up because Jonathan and

I are thinking about having a baby soon," Stephanie said.

"You're kidding." Casey stared at her with a blank expression.

"You and a baby?" Kara laughed. "No way."

Stephanie frowned. "What's so surprising about that? I can handle it. I've handled much more difficult things in my life before."

"Oh, sure." Liz nodded. "There was that broken nail back in September . . ."

"Don't forget the time someone stole her black leather belt and she had to wear a brown belt with black shoes," Eileen said.

Everyone started laughing.

"Come on, I'm serious," Stephanie said.

"Why do you want to have a baby so soon?" Kara asked.

Stephanie paused. Should she tell them why? To make her marriage feel more secure and real? To make sure she never flirted with another guy again? No, she couldn't admit that to anyone. She could barely admit it to herself.

"Because," Stephanie said. "Because I love Jonathan so much. Isn't it obvious?" She got to her feet, dropping the crust of her pizza into the nearly empty box. "In fact, I should get my stuff and get going or I'll be late."

She carried her gym bag into her old room and threw open the closet, where several boxes of her shoes and accessories were still stored. Then she leaned against the closet door and sighed. She'd been so anxious to move out of this dumpy room.

So why did it feel more like home than her apartment?

Bess dabbed beads of sweat off her forehead with a tissue. She peered at the mirror, trying to see if her makeup needed any work. Dress rehearsals were supposed to be as smooth and seamless as opening night. Bess wanted to be perfect. She quickly touched up her face powder and applied a fresh coat of lipstick. Then she headed backstage for her next scene.

From the wings, Bess peered out at the actors onstage. Everyone was doing a great job so far, especially Brian. Bess was starting to think that she might make it through opening night without major stage fright.

Daphne sauntered up to the prop table beside Bess, with something in her hand. She waved hello, brandishing a candy bar right in front of Bess's face. She began to unwrap the chocolate very slowly. She raised it to her mouth with one hand and took a bite while her other hand played with a few trinkets on the prop table.

She's doing this on purpose! Bess thought. Daphne thinks she can make me crack, so she can play Maggie on opening night. Well, she's wrong.

"Daphne, please don't mess with the props," Bess said quietly. Everyone knew the cardinal rule: Nobody except the prop person is to touch the prop table during a performance. Daphne ignored Bess's request.

"Mmm. I love hazelnuts in chocolate, don't

you?" Daphne asked seductively. "Want a bite?" She held the chocolate bar toward Bess.

"No, Daphne. No thanks," Bess said hurriedly. "I'm waiting for my cue."

"Gee, I'm surprised. I could have sworn you wouldn't have been able to resist." Daphne laughed and walked away.

Bess felt her eyes fill with tears as she glared at Daphne. Why did she have to be so mean? She was the only person who gave Bess a hard time about having bulimia, the only person who was cruel and insensitive enough to actually want to see Bess go back to her old habits.

"Bess, how are you feeling?" Justin asked, coming up behind her. "You looked great in the first act. I watched you from the lighting booth upstairs. You and Brian are awesome."

"Shouldn't you be doing the lights?" Bess asked.

"I came down to get a glass of water," Justin explained. "Besides, Hal has to know how to do everything himself. What if I called in sick or something? You'd still need light."

Bess looked him directly in the eye. "Don't you dare call in sick! Even if Hal does know what he's doing."

"I won't. I wouldn't miss opening night for anything," Justin promised. "Now, if I can just find a cup somewhere." He gazed at the prop table where several glasses were laid out.

"Don't touch those, Justin!" Bess said. "Doesn't anyone understand that the props are for the play?"

"Wait a second. What's that?" Justin leaned over the table. "Uh-oh, oh no. *No!*" he cried.

"What? What is it?" Bess asked. "Is something broken or—"

"There's a bomb!" Justin yelled, pointing at the table. "Everyone, look out! There's a bomb back here!" he shouted onto the stage.

Bess just caught a glimpse of a metal pipe with one end on fire lying on the prop table, before Justin grabbed her arm. "Get away, Bess!" he cried. "Move!"

As Justin pulled at her arm, Bess leaped away from the table. In midair she heard an ear-splitting boom!

CHAPTER 5

I say we open with a shot of everyone dancing; the music is loud—fun, fun, fun—and then we cut—*bam*—to Jason at the bar, before things started heating up." Michael's ideas for editing the Club Z video were dynamite.

"Yes, that's great! I agree. It'll catch the viewers' attention right off the bat." Nancy couldn't believe what she had just said. *Am I crazy or am I just worn out? I'm starting to agree with Michael Gianelli.*

"I like the juxtaposition of the two stages of the interview," Professor Trenton remarked. "It works. You get a sense of what it's like to own a club like that—the busy times and the dead times."

"The place was packed," Nancy said. "And we left when it was still early."

"Speaking of early," Professor Trenton said, glancing at his watch, "I should be getting home soon. I've got papers to grade before tomorrow."

"And I've got papers to *write,*" Nancy said, standing up. "We're signed up for the editing room here tomorrow."

"Do we know yet how long we have until the first show?" Michael asked. "We still have a few days to edit the piece before it airs, right?"

"Oh, yes." Professor Trenton chuckled. "I almost forgot. I found out that our weekly air time will be Thursday nights at eight, starting next week. How does that sound?"

"Uh, I don't think I can make it. I have a date for that night . . ." Michael began to protest.

Professor Trenton looked scandalized. Nancy was speechless, but only momentarily. "Are you saying that you—"

"Hey, I was joking. I was born to be on prime time," Michael said with a grin.

Nancy raised one eyebrow. "Right," she growled. "Very funny."

"Our first show will air one week from tomorrow," Professor Trenton said. "And you, Mr. Gianelli, had better improve your sense of humor before—"

Just then the studio's campus police scanner crackled. "Attention, all officers. Attention, Weston Police. We have an explosion at the Hewlitt Performing Arts Center. Repeat: an explosion has occurred at Hewlitt."

"An explosion?" Nancy felt her knees buckle.

"My . . . my friend Bess is at Hewlitt," she stammered. "She's in the play. Tonight they're having a dress rehearsal!"

"Let's go," Michael said. He tossed his notepad and pen onto the desk and grabbed the video camera from on top of the file cabinet. "Come on, Nancy—I'll drive."

"Let me know what you find!" Professor Trenton called after them.

Nancy rushed out of the building, feeling panicked. Michael steered her toward his VW.

"She'll be okay," he said as he opened the car door for her. "Calm down, Nancy. She'll be okay."

Nancy didn't say a word as Michael drove. As they approached the campus, Nancy could see that the Hewlitt building was still standing, intact. That was a good sign. Before Michael had even shifted the car into Park, Nancy had jumped out.

"Was anyone hurt?" she asked the person nearest her. "What happened?"

"No, no one was hurt," he said. "I heard it was a bomb."

"A bomb?" Michael repeated, with the camera rolling.

"That's what I heard—a small one—but I don't know anything else. Except no one got hurt."

"Thanks," Nancy said, and took off to find Bess. She slowly worked her way through the crowd. Students, their breath rising in white clouds in the cold night air, were eerily bathed in the flashing red and white lights of the fire trucks. They milled around, shocked and dismayed. Nancy kept overhearing bits of conversations as she searched for Bess.

"It was the boiler—"

"I heard the director was hit pretty bad—"

"They're saying it was a pipe bomb—"

"The police are questioning everyone—"

Nancy had to find Bess and sort this out. Maybe the first person she asked was wrong. Maybe people were hurt.

She glanced around and caught sight of Michael at a distance, filming the crowd. She saw him wave his hand to her and point in the direction of the backstage entrance. Bess must be there.

Police officers stood in knots near the building, interviewing students. Wisps of smoke were still coming out of the backstage door as the dark shapes of firefighters ran in and out.

Finally Nancy spotted Bess's long blond hair. She and Brian stood together, his arm around her shoulders holding her tightly. Nancy was glad to see that someone had given Bess a coat and a blanket to warm her.

"Bess! You're all right?" she called as she rushed over, wrapping Bess in a bear hug.

"I'm fine," Bess said, hugging Nancy back just as hard. "I'm fine."

"And you're okay, too?" she asked Brian from within the circle of her friend's arms.

"Yeah. Other than being freaked out, we're fine," Brian said.

Nancy finally felt secure enough to let Bess go.

Inside, she felt a heavy weight lift; Bess was all right.

"Where were you guys when it happened?" Nancy asked.

"I was lucky. I was onstage," Brian said. "But Bess was right next to it."

"What exactly was it?" Nancy asked. "I've heard just about every possible scenario from this crowd."

"It was a pipe bomb," Brian answered. "Small, but a bomb nonetheless."

Bess shuddered. "I was standing by the prop table, waiting for my cue. Daphne was there eating a candy bar—chocolate with hazelnuts—and she kept trying to get me to eat some. Finally she left and Justin came down to get a glass of water."

"Justin's the lighting designer for the play," Brian explained to Nancy.

"Justin saw the bomb on the prop table; I caught a glimpse of something burning. Then he grabbed my arm and pulled me away. There was this giant bang, and I went flying. Fortunately I landed in a pile of old stage curtains."

Suddenly Nancy wished Michael had gotten Bess and Brian on tape. The moment captured the terror as well as the relief. Where was he? She looked away from Bess to see if she could spot him, and sure enough, Mr. Nose-for-the-News was three feet away. He'd taped the entire thing.

A police officer approached them, led by Jeanne Glasseburg, the play's director. "Bess? Brian? The police need to ask you a few questions, okay?"

"Sure, Jeanne," Bess said. "See you later, Nancy, okay?"

"That's fine, Bess. Now that I know you're all right, I have some work to do." Nancy gestured toward Michael.

"Good luck," Bess said, with a knowing smile.

"Thanks, I may need it." Nancy returned Bess's smile and turned around to face Michael. What snide comment could he possibly make about this? she wondered. Probably something about putting her friends before her job. Well, he'd better be ready for a fight, if he thinks—

"I told you she'd be all right. But I know it doesn't mean anything until you actually see for yourself."

Once again Michael amazed Nancy. Just when she thought he'd be his typical jerk self, he was kind and even understanding.

"Yeah," Nancy agreed. "Thanks for driving me over. I think I would have run off the road if I'd tried."

The moment couldn't last.

"What, and miss the biggest news of the whole semester? You weren't in any shape to tape any of it. It's a good thing I was . . ."

Nancy had no energy to even listen to his bragging. She gazed around at the crowd and found herself smiling at Jake. He was walking toward her, no hat, no gloves, one hand stuck in his jacket pocket.

"Hey, Nancy. You guys here to do a story for the new TV show?" Jake asked. He looked cold.

Nancy nodded. "That, and to make sure Bess and everybody else are okay."

"Of course, they come first," Jake said. Nancy wasn't sure if he was teasing her or not. She shook the thought out of her head. *This is Jake you're talking to, not Michael.*

"You covering this for the *Wilder Times?*" Nancy asked. "Now that I'm not at the paper, you must get all the good assignments."

"Yeah, right." They both laughed. "I've been trying to get some information from the police, but they're not saying a word," Jake told her.

Michael leaped into the conversation. "Really? Let me see about that. The public has a right to know," he said, charging over to a group of uniformed and plainclothes officers.

Jake stared at Michael's back. "Is that Michael Gianelli?"

"Yep, that's Mr. Intensity. He's my cohost for *Headlines,*" Nancy said. "Not the easiest guy in the world to work with, but we're learning."

"Hmm. He's been in a few of my classes. Thinks a lot of himself," Jake said. "How are things, otherwise?"

"Pretty good," Nancy said. "Actually, there aren't many other things. This TV show seems to have taken over my life."

"I know what you mean." Jake nodded in sympathy. "The newspaper is taking up all my time since you're not there to share the burden—oh, and the glory."

Michael walked back over from the police with

a self-satisfied smirk. "They verified that the explosion was caused by a pipe bomb. So far, the cops have no idea who did it," Michael said.

"Hey, thanks for the tip," Jake said. "I guess I'd better do my own legwork from here on. See you later, Nancy. Thanks, Michael."

As Jake wandered into the crowd, Nancy turned to Michael. "Explain to me what a pipe bomb is, exactly," she said, stomping her feet to warm up. "Seems like you read about terrorists using them all the time."

"Right. A pipe bomb is what it sounds like, basically," Michael explained. "It's not very sophisticated, which is why you get a lot of nut cases trying to blow up the world with them. You take a metal tube, stuff it with gunpowder, and cap both ends. Light one end, and *vah-voom*."

"Who would want to bomb the theater?" Nancy wondered out loud, ignoring Michael's sound effects. "What could they possibly accomplish?"

"A bomb that size isn't going to damage the building. The police figure the point was to hurt— or maybe just scare—people, maybe just one particular person." Michael shrugged. "They have no idea who's responsible, so, if you'll excuse me"— the old, arrogant Michael was back—"I guess it's up to me to find out."

Nancy watched as he walked off. If nothing else, she thought, he sure knew how to go after—and get—information. Then again, if he'd stayed around to get her opinion, she could have told him a thing or two. He might have found it interesting that

Bess's understudy, Daphne Gillman, had attacked Bess just the night before. That sounded awfully suspicious when you also knew that Daphne was standing by the prop table moments before the bomb went off.

Nancy glanced across the lawn. The police had finished with Bess and Brian and had moved on to Daphne. Suddenly Nancy felt cold. Was Daphne really after Bess? The pepper spray incident had been no joke. Neither was a bomb.

Michael walked around Hewlitt, checking out the scene from all sides. Was this a general attack or had it been directed at one person? He had no idea. But if Nancy's friend had been the target, he wanted to find out who was after her. Not just for the sake of the story, which would play excellently on TV with or without an individual target, but for Nancy's sake. She'd been so shaken when she thought her friend's life was in jeopardy. He'd never imagined she could be so vulnerable. And he had stepped in and comforted her. Snap out of it, Gianelli, he ordered himself. This isn't the time for daydreaming. You have a story to do.

Michael gazed around the area and spotted a pretty girl in the outside lights. She had short blond hair and wore a Wilder Drama sweatshirt under her open pea coat. Since he had to interview someone, the person might as well be nice to look at.

He walked over to her, the video camera slung over his shoulder and a notepad and pen in hand. "Hi, are you in the play?" he asked.

"I helped build the sets," the woman replied. "My name's Marisa Bash."

"Hi, I'm Michael Gianelli. I'm doing a story for *Headlines,* the new campus TV show, and I need some background material. Can you help me?"

"Well, the play was written by Tennessee Williams, and it's about this intense Southern family . . ."

Michael smiled. "I meant background on the cast and crew, not the play itself."

"But it's a very good play," Marisa defended herself.

"Yes, it is," Michael agreed. "I read it last semester. But tonight I'm more concerned with reviewing what happened here than discussing the work of Tennessee Williams." If he wasn't careful, his snideness would lose him this interview.

"Okay," Marisa said. "What do you want to know?"

"Is there anyone who seems suspicious to you? Anyone who might have something against someone else?"

"Well, of course there is. Everyone is suspicious of her."

Michael's eyes widened. This sounded promising. "Who might that be?"

"Daphne Gillman, the lead's understudy."

"And, why, may I ask, is everyone suspicious of her?" Michael asked.

"For starters, she's obsessively jealous of Bess. Bess Marvin. She's the woman who plays the lead, Maggie. Daphne's always bringing her down, you know?" Marisa spoke very matter-of-factly. "And then there was the pepper-spray incident last night. Since Bess was right next to the bomb tonight, I guess that makes Daphne suspect number one."

"Wait, hold on," Michael said. "What pepper-spray incident?"

"You don't know?" Marisa didn't need an answer. "The way I heard it, Daphne jumped Bess right out here behind the theater. Daphne claimed she thought the figure she saw in the dark was going to attack *her.* So, out came the pepper spray and—*pssst*—right in Bess's face."

"Nasty," Michael commented.

"Yep, that's Daphne. She's so competitive about getting lead roles. When Bess got the part of Maggie, Daphne went ballistic."

"So, you think Daphne is out to hurt Bess so that Bess can't perform. Then in steps the understudy."

"Bingo. I'm not the only one who thinks so. I'm beyond just thinking anyway. I know Daphne's behind all this. You should talk to her, but she split right after the cops were done with her."

"Thanks, Marisa," Michael said. "You've been a great help."

It was getting colder, so the crowd had thinned out to just a few gapers. Michael had only one more question, but it would have to wait until he saw Nancy again. She must have known about Daphne. Why didn't she say something? A second question popped into his mind. What other information was Nancy keeping to herself?

* * *

"Radical Moves sounds incredible tonight!" Kara yelled over the loud music.

Ray looks even better, Montana thought, as she watched him strut across the stage. She imagined he was singing to her alone, even though about a hundred bodies filled the Club Z dance floor. Montana loved to dance, but right then her energy was focused on Ray, and only Ray.

"Don't drool," Nikki whispered in her ear.

"I'm not," Montana replied, feigning disgust.

The three girls were sitting at a table on an upper level of the club. Montana was trying to be nonchalant about her crush on Ray, but she wasn't hiding anything from anybody. She'd have to work on that.

The set finished with a romantic song, Ray's voice blending in perfect harmony with Karin's.

"They should get a recording contract," Nikki said.

"They will," Montana declared loyally. Nikki and Kara burst out laughing at her ultraserious tone. "Well, they will, someday."

"We're going to take a short break. Don't go away!" Ray announced to the crowd.

"Like we would," Montana said. "Like anyone would!"

"Hey, some of us have homework to do," Nikki said. "Which means I should get going."

"Likewise." Kara began to stand up.

Montana reached out to grab her friends' hands. "Don't leave yet, please," she begged. "I need you guys here for moral support."

Kara sat back down. "Why? Are you going to sing with the band or something?"

"I didn't know it was open-mike night," Nikki joked.

"You guys!" Montana whined. "I told you when we got here. Tonight's the night I'm going to ask Ray out." Montana looked over her shoulder to make sure no one had heard her.

"That's right, Montana, you did," Kara said with the utmost patience. "But you've been saying that for weeks—"

"And each time you chicken out," finished Nikki.

"Okay, okay! Just watch. I'm going to ask him right now," Montana declared, standing up.

"Kara, I think she means it this time," Nikki said.

"I'm impressed," Kara replied, sitting back in her chair.

"Don't be impressed yet," Montana told them. "Just be here when I get back." She straightened her black miniskirt and smoothed her flowered blouse.

"You're looking hot," Nikki said. "Just play it cool."

Play it cool, Montana repeated as she went downstairs to the main floor of the club. Easy enough for Nikki to say. She wasn't the one putting herself on the line. Montana stopped halfway down the spiral staircase and quickly drew her fingers through her curls. It's now or never, she told herself. Taking a deep breath, she threw back her shoulders and took the rest of the stairs like a queen.

Ray was heading into the hallway that led to club offices and pay phones. As Montana followed him, she felt her nerve slipping. Maybe I'll just make a phone call, she told herself, but before she could alter her course, someone beat her to the phone. She had no choice.

"Ray! I'm so glad I found you," Montana said, catching him just outside Jason's office. She reached out and put her hand on his arm. "That was a great first set."

"Thanks, Montana," Ray said. "Thanks for coming."

"Are you kidding? I don't think I've missed a single performance of Radical Moves."

"You've been there since the beginning, haven't you," Ray said with a smile. "I really appreciate that."

A small, awkward silence descended between them, which Montana took as her cue.

"Ray, there's something I've been wanting to ask you for a really long time." She took a deep breath. "Would you go out with me? Like, on a date? Because I'm crazy about you," Montana confessed.

"You are?" Ray bit his lip. "I don't think . . . I mean, I hadn't thought about . . ."

Montana's heart broke. Don't say anything more, she wanted to say, but Ray kept going.

"Montana, you're beautiful. And I'm really flattered that you like me." He took her hand and squeezed it firmly. "I like you, too. But as a friend, not more."

"Oh. S-ure," Montana stammered. "I understand."

"Montana, I'm sorry," Ray said. "Are you okay?"

"I'm fine!" Montana said, blinking back a tear. "Phew, it's smokey back here, you know?" She raised her hand to her eye and caught the tear just before it fell. "Look, I'd better go. I just wanted to say you guys were great. I'd stick around, but I've got a ton of homework to do. Good luck with your second set." Montana turned around and started walking. She felt she might die of embarrassment unless she got outside immediately. Ray wasn't interested in her—at all! She heard the door to Jason's office open and close behind her as Ray stepped inside.

Go upstairs, Montana coached herself. Get your coat—

"Montana?" Cory stepped away from the pay phone mounted on the wall. "Hey, I—"

Montana didn't hear another word. Cory'd been in the hall all that time, she realized, her mind flashing back on the figure who had reached the telephone before she had. It had been Cory. He'd overheard the whole thing! Not only had Ray rejected her, but there had been a witness to her humiliation. It was more than Montana could take in in one night.

She rushed past Cory without saying a word. She couldn't get out of Club Z fast enough.

CHAPTER 6

Bess rolled over in bed Thursday morning and pulled her down comforter up over her head. The last thing she wanted was to get out of bed. The world outside suddenly seemed too dangerous for her.

Visions from the last forty-eight hours crowded into her head. First Daphne had told the world about Bess's bulimia; then Daphne and her pepper spray; Daphne at the Student Union while Bess was putting up posters for her eating disorder support group; and Daphne at the prop table. Then the bomb went off. Bess shuddered, remembering the loud noise and how the stage floor shook underneath her feet.

Daphne, Daphne, Daphne. Bess couldn't get around the fact that Daphne had been everywhere, making her life miserable, and maybe even . . .

Bess's alarm clock shrieked in the morning air, bringing her back to the present. Her first class was in an hour, but Bess felt paralyzed, unable to move. She actually felt afraid to leave her bed, let alone her room. Whether it was Daphne or not, whoever had planted that bomb might try again. This time they could succeed.

I could use some breakfast, Bess suddenly thought. I wonder what's in the vending machine—besides M&M's? With everything so crazy lately, who cared what she ate, really?

Before she could think twice about cellophane-wrapped Fudge Delight brownies for breakfast, the telephone rang. "Divine intervention," Bess muttered as she got up to answer it.

"Hello, is this Bess?" a male voice asked.

"Yes. Who's this?" Bess asked.

"Justin. Justin Beckett? From the play—"

"Justin! Of course I know who you are," Bess said with a laugh. "I just didn't recognize your voice. I only got out of bed about ten seconds ago." She rubbed her eyes. "What's up?"

"I wanted to make sure you were all right," Justin said. "Last night was such a scene, I didn't get to say good night."

"No, I'm the one who should have found *you* to say good night." Bess sank into her desk chair. "Justin, you practically saved my life."

"Oh, no." Justin sounded embarrassed. "Not really. It wasn't like that—"

"It was," Bess insisted. "I totally owe you. If you hadn't seen that pipe bomb on the prop table, I could have been really hurt by the blast. Thanks for getting me out of the way."

"You're welcome," Justin said. "I'm just sorry it had to happen, you know?"

"I still can't believe it," Bess said. "Brian said someone out there must really hate Tennessee Williams."

"Huh?"

"It was a joke," Bess explained. "You know, Tennessee Williams wrote the play and someone doesn't like him, so they planted the bomb?" Justin didn't respond. "Well, I guess it's not so funny this morning."

"I just wanted you to know that you don't have to worry, Bess," Justin said. "Campus security and the police will be searching the building before tonight's dress rehearsal and before each peformance. And I'll make sure it's safe before you go out on stage again."

"My own private security guard, huh?" Bess laughed.

"You are the star of the show," Justin said. "Actually, Bess, I was wondering if maybe you wanted to go out—"

"Hold on a second, Justin—someone's at my door," Bess said, getting up to answer the loud knocking. She pulled open the door.

"Good morning. What are these flowers doing out here?" George held a bunch of yellow daisies.

"You didn't bring them?" Bess asked.

"No. I'm nice, but I'm not that nice," George joked.

Bess got back on the phone. "Hey, Justin? I'll talk to you tonight, okay? My cousin's here and—you didn't drop any flowers off here, did you?" she asked on a hunch.

"Flowers? No. Who sent them?" Justin asked.

"I don't know—a secret admirer, I guess. Hey, thanks again, Justin."

"Oh. Well, uh, you're welcome," Justin said, sounding slightly annoyed. "I'll see you tonight."

"Sure. See you." Bess hung up the phone and turned to George.

"Who was that?" George asked, making herself comfortable on Bess's bed.

"Justin. The guy who pushed me out of the way of the bomb last night," Bess explained.

"Did he send you these flowers?" George asked.

Bess laid the bouquet on top of her dresser. "No. I would have been surprised if he had. We're just friends."

"Then who did?" George asked.

Bess searched the bouquet for a card. "Last time my secret admirer sent roses."

"He's getting cheap," George said. "Not a good sign."

Bess frowned at her cousin. "Very funny." In the middle of the bouquet, she found a piece of paper tied to one of the stems.

"Well, what does it say?" asked George as Bess read the note silently.

" 'Hang in there! I'm rooting for you, from your secret admirer,' " Bess read out loud. "Then below it says, 'P.S. Don't worry, everything will be fine.' "

"So your secret admirer knows what happened last night," George pointed out. "Very interesting."

"George, it was on the news. Anyone who knows I'm in the play knows that I was there when the bomb exploded. The whole cast was there."

"Oh. Well, whoever this guy is, he's awfully supportive," George said. "I should have brought you flowers. I didn't think of that. But I did bring an idea. What you need is a day at the beach."

"Gee, thanks, George, but I don't know if I have time to go to Hawaii and back before tonight's rehearsal," Bess said. "But it's a nice idea."

"Not Hawaii, silly." George pulled out a brochure from her backpack. "There's a new spa right here in Weston. They sent coupons to students involved in sports: 'Come visit and bring a guest free!' We could go during lunch and be back for our three o'clock classes. You can be my 'guest free.' We'll get a massage, hang out in the sauna, try the heated pool—you know it should feel like a hot spring . . ."

"Not another word," Bess told her. "I'm there."

The flowers from her secret admirer were wonderful, but a little steam bath and aromatherapy seemed a much more enticing gift at the moment.

"Good morning!" Stephanie grinned and reached out to tickle Molly's tiny foot. "How are you, Molly? Hi, Jackie."

"Would you mind holding her, while I go get all the stuff?" Jackie asked, handing Stephanie the squirming bundle of baby.

"All what stuff?" Stephanie asked. She tried to cradle Molly in her arms the way she'd seen mothers do in magazines, but Molly had other ideas. She arched her back and threw her little body toward her mommy.

"You know, the things she'll need for the next few days," Jackie said, paying no mind to Molly's antics. "I'll be right back."

As Jackie disappeared down the hallway, Molly started kicking her legs frantically. As soon as Jackie was out of sight, she let out an ear-piercing wail.

"Molly, it's okay," Stephanie said, trying to soothe the baby by bobbing her up and down in her arms. "Molly, she'll be right back. Mommy's coming right back!"

Molly blinked once and then screamed again, right in Stephanie's face. The baby's eyes filled with tears, and her cheeks quickly turned a fiery red.

"Okay, maybe you want to come into the apartment and sit down with me. There, there," Stephanie said. This is getting out of hand and Jackie hadn't even left yet, Stephanie thought.

She suddenly remembered Jonathan's words when she had told him they'd be having a little guest for two days. It would be fun having a baby around, she'd said. "Fun? That isn't the word I would have used," Jonathan had replied.

"Oh, no. Is she pitching a fit?" Jackie came through the door with a huge baby bag slung over her shoulder, a folding portable crib in one hand, and a stroller in the other.

"Kind of," Stephanie said. "She didn't like it

73

when you left." She watched as Molly's crying mouth instantly turned into a smile when she spotted her mother.

"Don't take it personally," Jackie said, setting down her things. "She just doesn't know you or this place yet. But she adapts pretty quickly. Believe me, she'll be fine in a couple of minutes." She reached out, taking Molly from Stephanie. "Come on, honey, let's get your crib set up. Would you like that?" Jackie tickled Molly's stomach, and the baby laughed.

"I'll have to remember that one," Stephanie said, unfolding the crib.

"Speaking of remembering, I took the liberty of making out a list of things for you," Jackie said. "This tells you when you need to feed her, what you can feed her, how often she gets a bottle, when to put her down for the night . . . Well, you get the picture." Jackie handed Stephanie several sheets of notebook paper. "My phone number at the hotel is at the top. Call me anytime."

Stephanie stared at the list, her eyes glazing over. This was more complicated than most of her course syllabuses.

That was when it hit her. She'd told Jackie that she had a light schedule on Thursdays and Fridays, but she still had classes to attend. What would she do with the baby? Get a baby-sitter for the baby-sitter? She couldn't let someone else look after Molly without Jackie's approval, and she couldn't very well ask Jackie for names of baby-sitters. That meant she'd be bringing more than just a notebook to her art history lecture and French class.

"How does Molly do—you know—in crowds?" she asked Jackie as she stroked Molly's tiny foot again. "For instance . . . out shopping."

"She's fine. Just make sure she's had her bottle first," Jackie said. "She'll fall asleep for a few hours every afternoon—you might want to get any shopping done then. But watch out. When she gets tired, she can get really cranky."

"No problem," Stephanie said. "I'll make sure she gets plenty of rest." Of course, *I* might not, Stephanie thought. But she only had to look after Molly for two days—and Jonathan could help. Wasn't that what being parents was all about?

Nancy hurried down the sidewalk toward the Kappa house. The night before, Nancy had called Bess rather late, and they'd agreed to meet for lunch at Bess's sorority. Nancy wanted to make sure Bess was all right, plus she wanted to pick her brains for anything else she may have remembered about the bombing.

Maybe Bess would be interested in a date with Michael, Nancy mused. She'd only said a million times that he's gorgeous, and going out with the lead in *Cat on a Hot Tin Roof* would certainly suit his ego. Oh! Nancy realized that, of course, Bess could hardly go out on a date on opening night.

Nancy couldn't think of anyone to set him up with, and she was running out of time. The lucky woman would have to be very attractive and have a healthy ego and very tough skin.

"Nancy! Yo, Nancy!"

Nancy looked around and saw her roommate, Kara, on the front porch of the Beta fraternity house with her boyfriend, Tim Downing. Tim was looking good. Being a Beta seemed to agree with him, which was a relief since he'd almost dropped out of college after a disastrous pledge incident with the Alpha Delts. Of course, dating Kara seemed to agree with him, too.

"Hey, you guys!" Nancy called over. She began walking up the sidewalk toward the Beta house. "What's up?"

"I've been waiting for you with a message from Bess," Kara said. "She called this morning right after you left to tell you she can't meet you for lunch."

"Is she okay?" Nancy asked, suddenly afraid something had happened.

"She said something about hitting a spa for the day with George," Kara explained.

"Then she's doing better than I am right now," Nancy said, relieved. "What are you guys doing for lunch?"

"We just had lunch," Tim spoke up.

"Too bad. Well, I'm freezing and starving—"

"Wait, Nancy," Kara called out. She turned and spoke quietly to Tim, but not so quietly that Nancy didn't overhear.

"Nancy's doing a story on the bombing. Maybe you should tell her," Kara urged Tim.

"Tell me what?" Nancy asked.

"Come on up," Tim invited her. "It's warm inside, and there are probably some sandwiches left in the kitchen, if that will keep you from starving. Then we can talk."

Nancy settled on a grilled veggie and sprout sandwich. "You guys sure eat well," she said, amazed. "And I thought I'd have a choice of a hot dog or peanut butter."

Neither Kara nor Tim seemed in a joking mood. "Just teasing," Nancy explained. "No offense?"

"No," Tim said. "It's just that what I have to tell you is rather serious."

"Shoot." Nancy was suddenly filled with curiosity.

"There was an announcement at lunch," Tim began. "We Betas have been planning a big celebration for the fraternity's centennial this weekend. All fraternity alums have been invited and there's a blow-out party planned for tomorrow night, complete with fireworks. Only now some of the fireworks are missing."

"You're kidding," Nancy said. "Somebody stole them?"

"It looks that way. We had a few boxes of firecrackers—"

"But it's against the law to use fireworks in this state," Nancy interrupted.

"It is, unless you get a permit and have a professional set them off. We got all that, but we're not supposed to have the fireworks here beforehand. They should've been delivered to the Amazing

Cheru, who's putting on the show, but they showed up here instead." Tim paused to take a breath. "Well, the Amazing Cheru was supposed to come by and pick them up right away, only he hasn't had a chance yet. And now some of them are missing."

"Stealing the fireworks wouldn't be a fraternity prank, would it?" Nancy asked. "Don't you and the Zetas have a grudge match going?"

"Nope, not at all. That's all rumor." Tim shook his head.

Nancy paused to think. "So, are you thinking maybe somebody used the firecrackers to make last night's pipe bomb?" Nancy asked.

"Yep, I'm afraid that's what we're all thinking. I'd feel really horrible if our firecrackers had anything to do with it. *Really* horrible. So would the rest of the guys."

"Tim, I'm not asking you to rat on your frat brothers," Nancy said slowly. "But can you think of any Beta who might have something against someone in the play?"

"No," Tim said. "We were all here for lunch and we all talked about it. Someone would know if one of us was lying."

Nancy heard a loud shriek of laughter and glanced at the front door. Daphne was walking out, laughing with some friends.

"Do you know her?" Nancy asked, gesturing in Daphne's direction.

"Sure. We share a dining room with the Tau Omegas, so I know most of them," Tim said. "Her name's Daphne."

"You mean she lives in the Tau Omega house, next door?" Nancy asked.

Tim nodded. "Second floor, I think. It's kind of hard not to notice Daphne. I'd introduce you, but Daphne's never had the time of day for me."

"No sweat, Tim." Nancy stood up. "I can introduce myself. She's Bess's understudy in the play, and frankly, she's my number one suspect right now."

"Go for it, Nan," Kara cheered. "Give her the third degree. Get her confession on tape."

"Cut it out," Nancy said with a laugh.

"I wouldn't be surprised if Daphne had something to do with it. But I seriously doubt she knows anything about pipe bombs," Tim said.

"You may have a point. Well, here goes nothing." She walked out the door and across the porch toward Daphne and her friends. "Daphne? Do you have a second?" she asked.

Daphne gave her a cold, disdainful stare. "Do I know you?"

"Not yet. I'm Nancy Drew. I recognized you from last night. You're in *Cat on a Hot Tin Roof,* aren't you?" Nancy asked, feigning ignorance.

"Yes. And I recognize you, too. You're friends with Bess Marvin," Daphne said. "I saw you hugging her last night. Which means I don't have much to say to you." She turned back to her friends, and the whole group of them marched off.

Nancy turned to find that Tim and Kara had joined her.

"Friendly, isn't she?" she said as all three entered the house again. "Daphne obviously doesn't want to talk, but does that mean she's guilty or just rude?" No one had an answer. Nancy wondered how she would ever get Daphne to talk to her. She probably never would.

But maybe there was another way. Nancy knew one person who might be able to get through to Daphne. Michael was an amazing flirt. She hated to ask a favor of him, but this was something of an emergency. She'd just have to grit her teeth and ask him while they edited the Club Z piece. Too bad I can't get Daphne to be his blind date, Nancy thought wickedly.

Meanwhile, Nancy wasn't going to sit around waiting. "Hey, Tim," she said. "Do you mind showing me the firecrackers that didn't get stolen? It might help me out."

"Sure, c'mon," Tim said, heading for the basement door. "But don't expect this place to be neat."

"Don't worry," Nancy said. "I don't."

CHAPTER 7

"Montana? Is that you?"

"Shh!" Montana pulled the giant straw hat down on her head, so that its wide brim completely covered her face. Did Nikki have to announce her presence to everyone in Java Joe's? "Why don't you just use a megaphone? Of course it's me," Montana whispered.

Nikki and Kara sat down on either side of her. "Are you planning a trip to Mexico or something?" Nikki asked, peering under the brim of the hat. "I can't even see your eyes."

"Good," Montana said. "I don't want anyone to see my eyes, or any other part of me. I'm invisible, in case you didn't notice."

"Not to be contrary, but there's something about a giant straw hat, worn out of season, on a gray wintry day, not to mention in the middle of a crowded coffeehouse hundreds of miles from any decent beach, that makes you kind of conspicuous," Kara pointed out.

"The people at the next table barely have room to sit down," Nikki said, laughing.

Montana shifted in her chair and pressed the brim down on both sides, trying to take up less room. "I feel bad enough without you guys making fun of me."

"You're not still upset about last night, are you?" Nikki asked. "If Ray doesn't want to go out with you, it's his loss."

"Yeah. He's crazy, like I said before," Kara added. "You guys would be great together."

"I know!" Montana sighed. "That's what makes this so hard. I'm totally humiliated that he doesn't feel the same way."

"If I buy you a cappuccino, will you take off that silly hat?" Nikki said. "It doesn't help your chances of meeting another guy."

"I don't *want* to meet anyone else," Montana said.

"Sure you do," Kara told her. "You just don't know it yet." She looked up at Nikki. "Get her a double capp, stat. And here," she said, handing over a five-dollar bill, "get one for me, too. Cocoa on top. Then we'll talk."

As Nikki went up to the counter, Montana peered around the coffeehouse under the protection of her hat brim. She didn't see anyone she knew. Even more important, she didn't see Ray or

Cory. She hoped they were rehearsing that afternoon. Then chances were they wouldn't show up at Java Joe's. But just thinking of Ray singing at rehearsal was enough to make Montana feel like moving to Antarctica—permanently.

"Here you go!" Nikki set a steaming cup of coffee and froth in front of Montana and handed one to Kara. She lifted her own in a toast. "Drink up. Montana, cheer up. Life's not over. Not as long as you have us around."

"Thanks, but you're not exactly dating material," Montana retorted.

"So, you admit it," Nikki challenged. "You do want to meet someone new."

Ignoring Nikki's comment, Montana stirred sugar into her coffee and took a sip. "Ah, coffee!" She sighed. "Okay, so maybe I am overreacting." She lifted the hat off her head and shook out her long blond curls.

"She lives!" Kara cried.

"But if you guys really want to help me," Montana said, "you'll take over our radio show Saturday and interview Ray and Cory for me."

"You're the one who asked them to be on the show! You have to be there," Nikki said.

"I can't," Montana protested. "I can't face either of those guys right now. Now? What am I saying? I never want to see them again, ever."

"Yes, you do," Kara said. "Or are you going to skip every Radical Moves appearance from now on? You'll miss all the best parties that way."

Montana took another sip of her coffee. "I don't

care. As far as I'm concerned, I've seen that band more than enough."

"Right." Kara nodded. "They're getting boring. Bor-ing! Same old songs. Same old singers."

"Lousy stage presence," Nikki added. "And that lead singer—what's his name? Roy? Ray?—couldn't sing 'Do, Re, Mi' on key."

"Okay, okay. You made your point," Montana said with a laugh. "Radical Moves is a really good band, and I hope they're really successful. But I'm *not* doing the interview. You guys are."

"All right, if you insist." Kara sighed dreamily. "But I'm going to hate being so close to two such gorgeous guys for an hour. Just hate it."

"Come on, fun's over," Nikki announced. "Drink up and let's head over to the radio station. While we're there, we can make a list of questions for Saturday. You can help us out with that, right?"

"Sure," Montana agreed. "This question is for you, Ray Johansson: are you crazy, or what, turning down the great Montana Smith?"

"That's the spirit," Kara said.

The three of them stood up and started gathering their belongings. Montana put her leather backpack over her shoulder and juggled the giant straw hat in one hand and her coffee in the other. She walked out the door behind Kara, and held it for Nikki with her foot. Two customers were coming in, so she held the door for them, too, without even looking up.

"Thanks, Montana," Cory said. "You know, Ray, maybe we should tip her."

"Er, uh, yeah," Ray mumbled.

Montana froze in place. She wanted to run away, but her feet wouldn't move. "Uh, you're welcome," she muttered. Kara grabbed Montana by the sleeve of her coat and pulled her out of the doorway. The closing door neatly clipped Ray's shoulder.

"Smooth," Montana said, shaking her head as they began walking across campus. "Real smooth."

"If it's any consolation, he was just as embarrassed as you were," Kara said.

Montana jammed the straw hat back on her head. "It isn't."

"Good news," Michael said as he strolled into the *Headlines* office he and Nancy shared. "Trenton okayed changing our first show from student entrepreneurs to the bombing."

"All right! So, have you found the bomber yet?" Nancy asked teasingly.

"Have *you?*" Michael challenged.

"I didn't realize this was a competition," Nancy said. "Or should I just assume that everything's a competition with you?"

"Speaking of which, have you found the perfect date for me yet?" Michael asked. "Because our date's coming up fast—tomorrow night."

"No, I haven't found her yet," Nancy admitted, irritated. "And I'm not sure if she exists!" She changed her tone to one that was soft and reassuring. "But don't worry, I won't give up. Just as I'm not giving up on the two of us trying to work together as a team." She smiled at Michael.

"Wait a second. I think I'm hurt." Michael arched one eyebrow. "Are you saying I'm difficult?"

"Difficult? Yes. But that's all right. I like challenges," Nancy said with a shrug.

"Good," Michael replied. "So do I. Now, do you want to hear what I've found out?"

"I thought you'd never ask," Nancy said.

"My source in the police department told me that the gunpowder in the pipe bomb came from a firecracker. The lab found traces of the wrappers. Your turn."

"First," she began, "I have a question. How did you ever get a *source* in the police department? They don't give out information to anybody when they're conducting an investigation, much less to a college student."

"What can I say? I'm irresistible." Michael shrugged.

Nancy rolled her eyes. "To the police? No, really. Tell me."

"Simple, standard journalism. If you ask the right questions, and you ask them often enough, eventually you get some answers," Michael said smugly.

Nancy didn't buy it, but had she really expected a straight answer? "Okay, however you found out about the firecracker wrappers, it's rather interesting when you also know that some firecrackers were stolen from the Beta house recently," Nancy said nonchalantly.

"Stolen?" Michael nearly leaped out of his chair.

"You're kidding. How? What were they doing there in the first place? It's completely illegal."

"I know that," Nancy said. "They bought them for a huge celebration, and they'd gotten the permit and hired a pro to do the honors, but the firecrackers got delivered to the frat house by mistake. They were locked in a closet in the basement. Somebody jimmied the lock."

"When were they stolen? Before the explosion, I'm guessing?" Michael asked.

"Brilliant deduction, Watson," Nancy said. "The guys at Beta aren't sure when, but it can't be a coincidence. We find the thief and we find the bomber."

"I agree, but unless we can match the stolen firecrackers with the scraps of wrappers found in the bomb, the connection is circumstantial. It won't hold up in court, Sherlock."

Nancy felt victorious, and Michael didn't even realize he'd just lost a battle: in the investigation department, he had just become Dr. Watson to her Sherlock Holmes. As it should be, she thought.

"Well, maybe your *source* can tell you what brand of fireworks they found in the bomb and we can see if it's the same as the missing ones from Beta," she said, tapping her fingernails against the desktop. "But we're still left with *who*. Who did it?"

"What about that Daphne woman? The one who pepper-sprayed your friend Bess?"

"How do you know about that?" Nancy asked.

She hadn't told him about either Daphne or the pepper-spray incident, yet.

"Sources," Michael reminded her. "The police aren't my only source, you know. I just want to know why you felt it necessary to withhold this rather important piece of information from me." He didn't let Nancy say anything in her defense. "And it just makes me wonder what other secrets you may have tucked inside that beaut—er, head of yours." Michael cringed.

Beautiful, hmm? Nancy'd have to think about that one later. Meanwhile, Michael was so embarrassed, Nancy knew she was off the hook. She could simply ignore his questions and focus on Daphne. Then she suddenly realized that she might not have to ask her favor of Michael after all.

"Have you talked to Daphne yet?" Nancy asked.

"No, just heard about her," Michael replied. "But I'd love to interview her."

"Hmm," Nancy murmured. "Actually, she lives in the Tau Omega sorority, right next door to the Betas. She eats her meals at the fraternity—some of them, anyway," Nancy said. "So she could have known about the firecrackers. She knows I'm Bess's friend and won't have anything to do with me."

"No problem." Michael tapped his chest. "I'll get her talking."

"Just like your police source?" Nancy asked.

"Not exactly. My police source is a man," Michael said. "I think this assignment calls for turning on the old Gianelli charm—"

"Yeah, yeah. Spare me the details," Nancy said. "Just see what you can find out, okay?"

"Shh," Stephanie whispered. "Shh." Unfortunately, Molly was paying as much attention to Stephanie as Stephanie was paying to her art history professor. Stephanie tried moving Molly from one arm to the other, and in the process her pen, notebook, and Molly's bottle wound up on the floor for the umpteenth time.

It is impossible to take notes on a lecture while holding a fidgety baby, Stephanie concluded. Everything had been fine until about five minutes ago, when Molly had stopped sleeping and started experimenting with her voice.

"La la," she said. "Eeeeeee . . ."

The student in front of Stephanie turned around and cleared his throat. "Do you mind?" he growled.

"She's an infant," Stephanie said. "Give her a break. Shh, little Molly, shh. We're learning about Van Gogh."

Molly looked up at her with watery brown eyes. Stephanie rubbed her foot, which usually delighted the little imp. Molly smiled. YESSSS! Stephanie cried triumphantly—and silently.

"And perhaps the most important thing to remember about Van Gogh's work," Professor Ringhals said, "is—"

"Aieeee!" Molly screamed.

The whole row in front of Stephanie turned around to glare at her.

"Haven't you ever seen a baby before?" she said.

"Seeing is fine. Hearing is another!" one woman said.

"We're missing the whole lecture," another student complained.

"Fine. Molly prefers Rembrandt anyway!" Stephanie stood up and quietly tried to gather their belongings. But just as she bent down to grab the strap of the baby bag, Molly arched her back and bumped her head against the arm of the chair. "Let me kiss it and make it better," Stephanie cooed, pressing her lips to Molly's head.

More startled than hurt, Molly let out a terrifying "Waaahhhhhh!"

"Excuse me," Professor Ringhals said, raising her voice and lowering her reading glasses. She peered in Stephanie's direction. "Is there a problem?"

"No, uh, no problem. Sorry for the distraction." Stephanie picked up the last of her things and hurried out into the hallway.

Molly stopped crying as soon as they left the lecture hall. "It's okay, honey," Stephanie said. "I thought it was boring, too."

Okay, so art history was over for the day. Stephanie's only remaining class was advanced French at three o'clock. That shouldn't be so bad since Thursdays were devoted to conversation. They could talk about almost anything, as long as they talked about it in French. Stephanie opened her appointment book and flipped through it to check on the day's homework assignment. "Exam—1/4 of grade" was written in giant red letters in the square for that date.

Stephanie nearly dropped the baby. An exam? She'd forgotten all about it.

She ran as best as she could to the nearest pay phone. With her hands full of baby and baby equipment, she couldn't search for a quarter. "Don't tell your mother," she cautioned Molly as she set her on the hallway floor. Molly, however, didn't care for the cold, hard tile and sent up the message loud and clear. At least by the time Stephanie had found a quarter and dialed Berrigan's Department Store, Molly was back in her arms and content.

"Jonathan? It's me," Stephanie said when she was transferred to his direct line. "Is there any way you could take care of Molly this afternoon? Please?"

Jonathan laughed. "Stephanie, I can't just leave work in the middle of the day."

"Don't laugh at me," Stephanie said as Molly began to whimper. "I'm having a really hard day."

"Sorry to hear that. I am, too," Jonathan said.

"I forgot I have a French test at three o'clock. Molly made so much noise in my last class, there's no way I can bring her to an exam," Stephanie explained.

"Maybe the professor will let you take it another time," Jonathan suggested.

"You don't know Professor LaGrange. He doesn't accept excuses," Stephanie said. "You could die and he'd still yell at you—in French—for missing class." Molly finally seemed to settle down, resting her head on Stephanie's shoulder and blinking sleepily. She was so cute when she wasn't screaming.

"I don't know what you can do," Jonathan said. "Maybe somebody at Thayer—"

"Jonathan, I can't ask anyone else but you. I promised Jackie that *we'd* take care of Molly," Stephanie cried. "Nobody else."

"Stephanie, you're the one who promised her. *I* didn't."

"Jonathan! Can't you put her crib in your office?" Stephanie whined. "It's only for a few hours."

"That won't work," Jonanthan said. "We're short-staffed. I've really got to get back to the floor. I'll see you tonight." He quickly hung up the phone.

Stephanie stood in the hallway, listening to the dial tone. She'd have to skip the exam and get an F. Thanks to Jonathan, her GPA was going to plummet. Some help he'd be as a father!

"Come on, Molly. Let's go home and watch the soaps," Stephanie said, picking up the baby bag. "Or *Sesame Street*, whichever looks better."

That evening Nancy and Michael met in the auditorium at Hewlitt before the cast and crew finished the interrupted rehearsal of the night before. There were a surprising number of police—both onstage and in the house—which meant that Nancy didn't have to worry about Bess and could concentrate on the investigation.

"So this is where it happened," Michael stated.

Nancy nodded. "Actually, back there—backstage." They hadn't been able to see the crime scene the night before because the police were gathering evidence. Even Michael's famous source hadn't gotten them in.

Every member of the cast and crew—including Daphne—would have to be at the rehearsal. Nancy was hoping to find someone who'd actually seen something while Michael worked his magic on Daphne, but only a few crew members were around finishing up the repairs to the sets.

"Hi," Michael greeted a thin student with small, round glasses and brown hair who was standing near them.

"Are you guys working for the newspaper?" the guy asked.

"Naw," Michael said.

"The TV station," Nancy told him. "You're Justin, right? You're the one who saved Bess."

He nodded, looking sort of shy. "I saw the bomb, so I pushed her away. It was no big deal. Anyone could have done it."

"Maybe, but she's lucky you were there," Nancy said.

"Yeah, I guess she was," Justin said, looking thoughtful.

"We thought we'd just look around—" Michael began.

"I can show you around," Justin offered. "I finished checking the lights. That's my job. I'm the lighting director."

"Okay," Nancy agreed. "Thanks."

Michael hopped up on the stage, then turned to give Nancy a hand up, but she was already standing beside him onstage.

"Nice move," Michael said slowly as Justin started describing the night before.

"Bess was waiting in the wings," Justin said. "I'd say she was standing right about there." He pointed to a spot on the floor. "I don't know what made me look at the prop table, but I did. The pipe was burning at one end and sort of rolling toward me. I didn't know what to do, except that I had to get Bess out of there. I grabbed her arm and sort of shoved her away. She landed over there, on top of those old curtains."

Michael was taking notes. "So you were the only one who saw the bomb before it went off?"

"I don't know," Justin said. "I guess so. It was a good thing I did, too, or Bess might have been really hurt. Maybe even killed. I talked to her this morning and she was still very upset. She couldn't get it out of her mind. I'm just really glad I could help. If anything happened to Bess, I'd never forgive myself."

Nancy wondered whether Bess knew that Justin was so attached to her. As far as she knew, they weren't close friends—not like Bess and Brian. Maybe they'd grown closer. If anything could bring two people together, it was surviving a disaster.

"Bess was really grateful." Justin pushed the glasses up on the bridge of his nose. "I guess she feels she owes me her life. But I don't feel that way."

"You're just glad you were in the right place at the right time?" Nancy asked.

"Exactly." Justin crooked a thumb at his chest. "I mean, look at me. I'm not exactly hero material. But I saw that bomb and had to do something. It all came down to a split second." He snapped his fingers.

Nancy exchanged a bemused glance with Michael. Justin was laying it on a little thick. He was obviously enjoying the attention.

"Thanks, Justin," Michael said. "Nancy, how about we check out the dressing rooms next?"

"What do you think you'll find there?" Justin asked.

"We're not sure. But we might find a clue," Nancy explained.

"Oh, yeah. They're back there. I'll show you." Justin led them through the backstage area and down a hall. "Here's the men's, and here's the women's."

"Great. Thanks a lot, Justin. I think we can take it from here," Michael told him.

"Really? Well, if you have any questions, come find me," Justin said.

"Will do," Michael assured him. He waited until he was sure Justin was out of earshot before asking Nancy which one she wanted to try first.

"Women's, of course, since Daphne's our prime suspect. Let's see if she has anything in here." Nancy pushed the door open. Inside, several small tables and a long counter in front of a mirror were covered with stage makeup. A row of large, oversize lockers were lined up along one wall, each one labeled with the actor's name.

"Here's Bess's locker." Michael peered inside. "Why don't they lock these things?"

"I guess the building's usually locked." Nancy shrugged as she looked for Daphne's locker. "Here it is," she said. "It's empty, except for a couple of old lipsticks—"

"Excuse me. What are you doing in here?"

Nancy whirled around to find Daphne standing behind her, hands on her hips. She had a large bag over her shoulder, which she dropped onto the bench in front of her locker.

"Hi, Daphne!" Nancy said in a falsely cheerful voice. "How's it going?"

"Fine. Now, why are you here? And why is a man in the women's dressing room?" Daphne asked.

"He's confused," Nancy said.

"Very funny," Michael muttered. Then he turned to Daphne with a giant smile. "Hi, I'm Michael Gianelli. . . ."

CHAPTER 8

So, you're Daphne. I've heard a lot about you," Michael said in his most flirtatious voice. "I can't believe I'm finally getting a chance to meet you."

"What's that supposed to mean?" Daphne asked.

"Nothing." Michael laughed. "I just wanted to meet you, that's all. I understand that the success of almost every drama department production relies on your talents."

He watched as Nancy quietly circled the dressing room and tried to peek inside Daphne's bag.

"Yes, it's true," Daphne said, slowly shaking her hair back. "But theater types are so competitive. I'm surprised anyone admitted it."

"You must know this theater inside and out. I'm trying to do a story about the bombing—for Wilder's new TV news show, *Headlines*. Do you think I could interview you?"

"Sure!" Daphne gushed. "I could tell you a thing or two. You mean, on camera, right?"

"I've got it right here. Now, let's see. . . ." Michael glanced at Nancy. She signaled him that she wanted to get a look inside Daphne's bag. "How about we tape you onstage—where you belong."

"Perfect," Daphne said. "But we need to hurry, before the others show up."

They were halfway out the door when Daphne realized that Nancy wasn't following them. "Aren't you coming?" she asked in a snooty voice. "Don't you run the camera or something?"

"I'll be right there," Nancy promised. "I just need to use the bathroom. You go ahead."

Nancy would have only a few minutes before the rest of the cast arrived. Michael had to hustle Daphne out of there.

"Come on, Daphne. I have a feeling this interview's going to go into overtime," Michael said, winking at her.

"So, who told you that my talent carries all the shows?" Daphne asked as they walked down the hall toward the stage.

"I'm afraid I've already said too much." Michael's voice was dripping with sweetness. "A journalist has to keep his sources confidential." They laughed as if they'd just shared a joke.

Suddenly Daphne stopped. "Before I go on camera, I should really touch up my makeup."

"You look fine," Michael told her. "You look *gorgeous.*"

"Thanks. But I'd feel better if I freshened my lipstick. People can look *so* washed out on TV," Daphne said, turning around and walking back toward the dressing room.

"But we can have Justin use muted lights!" Michael called to her. If he couldn't stop Daphne, at least he could make enough noise to warn Nancy that she was coming.

"I wouldn't rely on Justin's talent," Daphne said. "He's always got his head in the clouds."

"But we have to get this done before the other cast members show up," Michael protested.

"We can't start without your assistant, can we?" Daphne said as she pushed the dressing room door open. She stopped dead in her tracks when she saw Nancy standing by her locker, holding a wooden box in her hand. Michael cringed at both the sight of Nancy caught red-handed and the fact that she must have heard Daphne call her his assistant.

"What are you doing with that?" Daphne asked, fury sounding in her voice.

"I could ask the same question of you." Nancy spat the words at Daphne.

"You went through my bag?" Daphne was incredulous. "Why? What gives you the right?"

"Daphne, I'm truly sorry if I've invaded your privacy," Nancy said. "But I have a bigger problem. Someone tried to injure one of my best friends in a bomb blast last night. And the gunpowder used in that bomb came in a box just like this one."

"Give me my box back and get out of here before I call security," Daphne demanded.

"I don't think so," Michael said.

"This box matches the ones filled with fireworks in the basement of the Beta house," Nancy continued. "But some of the boxes were stolen, and the gunpowder from the fireworks wound up in last night's pipe bomb. Since you claim it's your box, Daphne, I think it's we who should be calling security."

"Do you want to tell us where you got the box, Daphne?" Michael asked her gently.

"I found it backstage last night, not that it's any of your business. It was in a trash can." Daphne shrugged.

"And how often do you go through the trash?" Nancy asked. "You don't strike me as the type."

"The box was sitting on top. I thought it was cool," Daphne said. "I was going to store CDs in it."

"Then why are you still carrying it around with you?" Nancy demanded. "Because one of your sorority sisters might see it if you left it in your room? That might raise a few questions, since all the Tau Omegas know about the theft at the Beta house next door."

"Hey, I didn't know what it was," Daphne said. "It looked cool, that's all. So I took it. There's nothing on there that says it contains firecrackers, so how would I know that's what it was?"

"You would certainly know it if you were the one to steal them," Nancy said, amazed at

Daphne's weak attempt to wriggle out of her predicament. She would have expected more from the great actress. Then again, Kara's boyfriend Tim had said that she wasn't the brightest star in the universe.

Daphne was finally beginning to see the trouble she was in. "Look, whoever planted the bomb must have tossed the box after he was done. I found it. That doesn't make me guilty."

"True," Michael said. "But Bess saw you at the prop table, right before the explosion."

"Yeah, so?" She glared at him. "She's just mad because I was standing there eating a candy bar. Unless eating chocolate is a federal offense, I'd like to go now, officers." She grabbed the box from Nancy's hands.

"Is this the only box you found?" Nancy asked her.

"Yes. Now, get lost already!" Daphne cried.

"Two boxes were stolen," Nancy said, her forehead creased with concern. "Which means one of them might still be out there, with the bomber."

"Not my problem." Daphne stuffed the box into her bag.

"If another bomb goes off, it just could be," Michael told her angrily. "You should turn that box over to the police, so they can use it to track the bomber. Or would you like to see innocent people get hurt? Do you enjoy stuff like that?"

"Of course not. Don't be ridiculous." Daphne looked up at both of them. "I'm not a monster, you know."

"Oh, yeah? Prove it," Michael said. He and Nancy walked out, leaving Daphne speechless.

Bess put on a coat of lip balm and slung her purse over her shoulder. She was relieved that the final dress rehearsal was over. It had gone fairly well, considering the heavy layer of free-floating anxiety that hung in the air.

If it hadn't been for the sublime three hours she and George had spent at the spa, Bess would have been a basket case. As they left, Bess swore that if she ever came into extra money, she'd buy the two of them a membership.

Jeanne Glasseburg had called the entire cast and crew together before beginning rehearsal to reassure them that the building had been searched, and would continue to be searched every day. But Bess was still worried. Even if the pepper spray had been an accident, planting a bomb inside the theater wasn't.

"Good night, Jeanne," she called to the director, who was going over a scene with Brian.

"Good night, Bess. Be safe," Jeanne said with a wave. "You'll be great tomorrow night."

"Thanks."

"I'll call you a little later, Bess," Brian said.

"Not too late! I need my beauty sleep," Bess told him.

"Good night, everybody!" She waved to a group of crew members on the stage.

"Good night!" they called back.

Bess walked out the front door of Hewlitt and

was halfway down the steps when she heard a voice behind her.

"You looked really wooden today."

Bess whirled around. Daphne was standing on the steps. In the moonlight, her body cast a shadow across Bess's path.

"Oh, are you doing reviews now?" Bess asked.

"You'll need to put more emotion into the part tomorrow if you want to make it work," Daphne said.

"I was tense, Daphne. Everyone was." Bess massaged her neck. "With good reason, after what happened yesterday."

"Get over it already," Daphne said. "You're all right, aren't you? You can go on with your precious performance tomorrow night."

"Yes, I can. Thank you for reminding me. I'll be going now," Bess said. "Unless you'd like to spray me with something before I leave?"

"Don't be ridiculous. But I do have something to say to you." Daphne walked down the steps and stood in front of Bess. "I've had it with your constant accusations."

"What accusations?" Bess asked incredulously.

"First, the police asked me if I was involved with the bomb. As if I would be. Then your friend with her cute brute of a sidekick and their little TV camera interrogated me today after searching my bag. A regular junior police force they are, all by themselves." Daphne shook her head. "Believe me, Bess. You're not *that* important to me. If I wanted to get rid of you? I could. Like that." She snapped her fingers.

"You've been watching too many bad cops and robbers films, Daphne. What next? Will you rub out my family?" Bess laughed. "As you said, I'm fine and I can get on with the show tomorrow. So, stay out of my way." Bess took a step around her understudy.

Daphne glared at her. "Just quit thinking that I'm behind any of this. I'm not. And if you try to pin it on me, you'll regret it."

"Whatever you say, Daphne." Bess shrugged. "As long as the security guard's nearby . . ." She glanced back into the lobby of Hewlitt and saw not one, but two, guards on duty. "I'm not going to worry about you. But just to be on the safe side, I think I'll go back inside and see if someone's walking my way. It seems like our little chat is over."

Bess went back into Hewlitt and nearly bumped right into Marisa Bash. "Hey, Marisa, are you walking across campus?" she asked.

"Yeah, I was just on my way."

"Mind if I join you? I could use some company, if that's okay," Bess said. "I live in Jamison."

"Perfect—I live right near there," Marisa said.

There was no sign of Daphne as Bess and Marisa descended the steps and set off.

"After that bomb last night, I've been spooked about going anywhere by myself," Marisa confessed. "You must be feeling even worse."

"Why do you say that?" Bess asked. "It was a frightening experience for everyone."

"Yeah, but you were the target—weren't you? That's what I've heard. Daphne's flipped and she's going after you," Marisa explained.

"So, that's the word." Bess let the news sink in. "Frankly, Marisa, I don't know if I was the target or not. And I don't know if Daphne had anything to do with it either."

"Hmm." Marisa thought silently for a few steps. "You know, Bess, it was less scary when I could believe that it was just meant for you. Now I don't know."

"Don't sweat it, Marisa," Bess said reassuringly. They stopped in front of Jamison Hall for a minute. "I hate feeling scared. Who doesn't? It's as if we're powerless, you know?"

Marisa nodded. "I guess all we can do is go on with our lives."

"Right." Bess smiled. "As someone said to me recently, 'Get over it already. You're all right, aren't you?' "

Stephanie put her head on her pillow at about 6:30 A.M., Friday morning, and sighed. She'd never felt so tired in her entire life.

Molly had slept through the night—if you counted waking up at 4:30 A.M. as waking up in the morning. The baby had been raring to go, and it had taken Stephanie nearly two hours of playing with her and cuddling to coax her back to sleep.

Being back in bed felt wonderful. Stephanie couldn't wait to catch a little catnap before—

"BRRRRINNNGGG!" the alarm beside the bed

blared in her ear. Stephanie pounded the snooze button with her fist.

But the noise had already roused Molly, who was sounding her own alarm. Stephanie lifted her head an inch off the pillow in an attempt to get up.

Jonathan had just gotten out of bed and was pulling on his robe. Why was she knocking herself out to do everything? Jonathan had slept through the night. He was well rested. *He* didn't have giant circles under his eyes. Besides, he hadn't pitched in at all yet. Wasn't it his turn to see to Molly?

"Jonathan," Stephanie mumbled.

"Good morning," Jonathan said in a cheerful voice. "Molly sounds upset. Maybe you should check on her."

Stephanie frowned. "Why don't you check on her? You're up," she pointed out, pulling the covers up to her chin.

"I don't have time," Jonathan said.

"Jonathan, it's six-thirty in the morning. What else do you have to do?" Stephanie asked.

"I have to get ready for work."

"I know, but can't you *please* watch her for a half hour, so I can get some sleep?" Stephanie asked.

"I can't," Jonathan said. "I have a meeting at seven-thirty, and I've got to shower, get dressed, have breakfast—"

"So?" Stephanie interrupted angrily. "Does that mean you can't go get Molly and hold her for fifteen minutes first? Fifteen minutes. That's all I'm asking. I'm exhausted and—"

"No. Sorry," Jonathan said, heading for the bathroom.

"Jonathan, you haven't helped me with Molly at all," Stephanie argued, getting out of bed. Molly's cries tapered off to whimpers. "You haven't done anything! And every time I ask you to help, you're too busy. Meanwhile, I missed an exam yesterday, and—"

"Stephanie, I'm busy. I'm really busy at work this week," Jonathan said. "That's why I didn't volunteer to take care of Molly. If you'd asked me before you made this commitment, I would have told you I couldn't help."

"Jackie needed our help," Stephanie said. "I was trying to be nice. And you weren't busy with work this morning at four-thirty when she woke up."

"Look, Stephanie, you're the one who said you'd take care of Molly. Not me. If you end up doing all the work, that's not really my fault!" He marched into the bathroom, turned on the shower, and slammed the door.

Stephanie glared at the closed door. "Thanks for the support," she muttered. What was the point of being married if you didn't help each other out? Would Jonathan act like this with their own children? Would he be too busy for them?

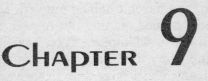

CHAPTER 9

"Hi, how's it going?" The lovely voice came from a long-legged woman in royal blue spandex bicycle shorts and a black leotard standing on the treadmill next to Michael's.

Michael had his nose buried in the front section of that Friday morning's *New York Times*. He looked over at the woman who had greeted him. Aside from her long legs, she had lusciously thick curly brown hair and looked as if she was in terrific shape.

"Hi," he replied with a nod, and went back to his newspaper.

"What are you reading?" she asked.

"The newspaper," he said. Wasn't it obvious?

"What's in the news?" She was persistent.

Michael stared at her. "Do you want to be more

specific, or should I just read the whole thing to you?"

"Never mind," she said, turning off her treadmill. "I was only trying to be friendly. I thought you were cute, until you opened your mouth." She hopped off the machine and walked to the other side of the gym.

"What are you doing?" asked Gus, who was running on the other side of Michael.

"Is there a stupid-question disease going around? I'm running, what does it look like?" Michael replied.

"I mean, why were you so rude to that gorgeous woman?" Gus asked.

"I'm busy," Michael said.

"Busy? Are you kidding me?" Gus laughed. "Since when are you too busy to notice a beautiful woman?"

Since Nancy. The words popped into Michael's head before he could stop them. He couldn't believe he'd been thinking about her since last night. They'd worked well together, or they were starting to. It was amazing how perfectly in sync they'd been while dealing with Daphne. And the night before, after the explosion. It was as though they each knew what the other was thinking before saying a word. He'd actually been having fun with her lately.

So what are you going to do about it, Gianelli? Michael asked himself. His plans for his future didn't include a coanchor. He knew what would happen. He and Nancy would make it onto network television, all right. They'd replace the *Good*

Morning show with the Michael G. and Nancy D. Show. They'd host parades and broadcast live from state fairs. He'd miss the story of the century because he'd be making plaid sugar cookies with Martha Stewart.

Not for this cowboy, Michael told himself. He thought of the greats—such as Edward R. Murrow and Walter Cronkite—and swore he'd be even better than they were. He had to break off this growing attachment to Nancy right away. He had to establish himself as the top reporter for *Headlines.* No more Mr. Nice Guy. He had a name to make for himself.

"Hey, Gus, are you busy tonight?" Michael asked.

"Not yet. Why?" Gus replied, stepping off the machine and rubbing his face with a towel.

"I just remembered," Michael said, slowing to an easy trot. "I made a bet with Nancy that I could fix her up with Mr. Right. She's supposedly finding Ms. Right for me. Tonight's the date, and I've given up."

Gus burst out laughing. "Why don't you guys just go out with each other?"

"Ha, ha. *Not.*" Michael shook his head emphatically, and sweat flew everywhere. "Anyway, she's not right for me."

"Oh, right. What was I thinking? She's only beautiful, talented, smart," Gus teased. "Why would you want to date *her?*"

"Look, do you want to go out with her or not? We're going to see *Cat on a Hot Tin Roof,*" Michael said.

"Sure." Gus shrugged. "Who am I to turn down playing Superman to Lois Lane."

"Don't call her that, especially to her face," Michael said. "She hates nicknames."

"Please. I've been on a date before," Gus scoffed. "I know how to act. Unlike *some* people I know."

Michael grabbed his water bottle, aimed, and fired.

Relax, Marvin. You're early, Bess told herself Friday as she walked into an empty meeting room in the Student Union.

What if nobody had seen her posters for the eating disorder support group? Or worse, what if they'd seen them and decided it wasn't worth their time? Not only did Bess want this group to succeed, she really needed the distraction this afternoon—just hours before her first performance as Maggie the Cat.

Bess paced back and forth in front of the windows, looking out at the crowded campus quad. She knew there were other women on campus who shared her problem. So where were they?

"Excuse me, is this the right room for the eating disorder group?"

Bess turned around. "Marisa?"

"Hi, Bess. Wow, I didn't expect to see you here," Marisa said, sliding into a chair at the circular table.

"And I didn't expect—well, I guess that's the whole point, huh?" Bess said with a nervous laugh. "We can't exactly help each other if we don't know we share a problem." She looked at Marisa thoughtfully. Marisa was so thin, and seemed so relaxed all the time, but Bess knew appearances could be deceiving. She'd hidden her own eating problem for weeks.

While she and Marisa chatted about opening night, the table gradually filled with other students—eight women and two men. At two o'clock, Bess started the meeting.

"Thanks for coming, everyone," she said, her voice a little shaky. "My name is Bess. I decided to start a support group because . . ." She paused, feeling embarrassed.

But what was there to feel embarrassed about, really? she asked herself. The only way to deal with her problem was to get it out in the open. She couldn't expect anyone else to talk freely unless she did the same.

"Because I got home the other night, and before I knew what I was doing, I had bought enough M&M's to feed a small country."

The room filled with nervous laughter.

"I've been there," one thin, dark-skinned woman said. A few heads nodded in agreement.

"I knew that if I didn't talk to my therapist right away, I would go right back to square one with my bulimia," Bess said. "Fortunately, she was home. But she can't always be there. And my friends . . . they try to understand, but they don't know what it feels like. So I started thinking that maybe there were other people on campus like me—others who need a friend who knows exactly where they're coming from. And I hope that's why you all showed up here today."

The room was quiet for a minute. Bess looked around at the others. "I guess the first thing we need to do is get to know each other. So, does anyone want to tell their story?" she prompted. "Or should I tell you mine?"

There was silence.

"It's hard to talk about," one woman spoke up quietly.

"I never realize how obsessed I am about food until I start talking about it," another woman added. "Then I'm like—what am I saying? It's *only* a bagel. You know?" She looked searchingly at Bess.

"Yeah, I do know," Bess said. "I guess when my bulimia started, food became something I could focus on. My life seemed so out of control. I needed something that made me feel better—at least for a while. If I focused on food, I'd never have to deal with what was really bothering me."

"What was that?" a male student asked.

"You sure you want to hear all this?" Bess asked.

"Go ahead," Marisa said.

Bess took a breath and told them about losing her boyfriend, Paul Cody, in a motorcycle accident. "Suddenly, everything drew me back to him and losing him. It sounds awful, but food gradually took his place."

For the next hour everyone around the table told their stories, revealed secrets, and reported victories. They exchanged tips on getting through the day and how to deal with friends and family. There were some tears and lots of laughter.

After it was over, and they'd planned their next meeting, Bess was glad she'd found the courage to follow through with her support group idea. She didn't feel half so alone or vulnerable anymore.

Nancy sat alone in her room, looking out the window at the chilly campus. She was ignoring the print on her computer screen.

It is absolutely impossible to find anyone I know to go out on a blind date with Michael Gianelli, she thought. I've tried everyone.

She went back to the computer to study the names of the friends and acquaintances she'd already called.

George had flat out refused.

"But, George," Nancy said. "Will's not here to go to the play with you. And I'm stuck on this blind double date with Michael. You can't give me one good reason why you won't say yes."

"I don't want to," George answered with a grin. "And if there is one thing I've learned so far in my college career, it's not to go out with anyone you have no interest in. Especially if you think he's a male-chauvinist macho throwback to the 1950s."

"That's not a good reason," Nancy complained.

"It's good enough for me," George said before hanging up to call Will in Chicago, where he was staying for the weekend.

Nancy had tried Nikki Bennett, but she said she

wasn't ready for that experience. Nancy had even tried Bess's sorority sister Soozie Beckerman. The two of them might even like each other. She'd forgotten that Soozie was seeing Nick O'Donnell now. It was too bad that Stephanie had gotten married.

Nancy moved on to the lists of students in her classes. She figured she knew a few women well enough to call. After all, they may not have heard about Michael's more negative points. The first three were either seeing someone or already had plans.

Then Nancy called Liz Richardson. They'd worked together on their first lit crit assignment.

"Liz," she said into the phone. "This is Nancy Drew. Remember, we—"

"Sure, Nancy, I remember you, I think." Liz sounded a little foggy.

Nancy didn't even get halfway through her explanation before Liz burst out laughing.

"Been there, done that, girl! Good luck!"

That was enough to put an end to the classmate approach. Too bad it's too late to put a personal ad in the *Wilder Times,* she thought. And that led her to a new idea. "Perfect," she said to the empty room. Nancy threw on her coat and bolted out the door.

The bookstore was hopping for a Friday afternoon, but at a glance Nancy saw that most of the crowds were in front of the mysteries, romances, and true crime books. I guess no one wants to read Kierkegaard or *Moby Dick* over the weekend, she thought. Would you? a voice from within asked her. I don't have to answer that, Nancy retorted. Besides, I'm not here for the books.

Nancy made her way to the psychology and self-help section, which was more populated than the urban-planning section, but less crowded than in front of the best-seller racks.

The Wilder bookstore had started up an informal dating service, consisting of two bulletin boards. One was marked Boys and the other, Girls. Someone had crossed out the word *girls* and written Women. Someone had tacked up a sign on the boys' board asking where the gay board was.

The idea was to write a description of yourself and tack it up. Girls on the girls' board and boys on the boys' board. If someone saw it and was interested, the person went to the information desk to get your phone number. That was supposed to be a caution against pranksters. But Nancy was an investigator. She'd take down names and use the campus phone book back in her room.

Oddly enough, only a few students lingered in front of either board. Nancy noted that they weren't all geeks, either, and then chastised herself for such an uncharitable thought.

Right away, one card caught Nancy's eye.

"Mackin Walsh, sophmore. Medium tall, with long red hair and a wry sense of humor. G.P.A. 3.0."

Nancy had met Mackin at one of Bess's sorority affairs. She seemed like a girl who might be able to hold her own, so down went her name in Nancy's notebook. She read through what seemed an ocean

of "dying to know you," "beautiful bombshell—
honestly," and "looking for fun," before she felt a
tap on her shoulder.

"Unless you've had a change of heart, Nancy, I
think you're looking at the wrong board."

Nancy spun around and was relieved to see the
only person on campus who might halfway understand what she was doing there.

"Don't say it, I know," Jake Collins said, with a
smile. "You're not looking for youself. You're
looking for a friend. Or maybe you're doing an
exposé for *Headlines*. What, the bombing wasn't
big enough news for you guys?"

"Stop already, Jake." Nancy laughed. "It's worse
than you think." She explained the blind date challenge with Michael—leaving out, of course, that
Michael's assessment of Jake was what had started
the whole thing.

"Ah, then, you definitely need a man's point of
view," Jake said. "Let's see who we have here.
Jeanine LaMay—I know her. She's far too nice to
set up with Mr. Tough Broadcast Journalist. Sara
Ann Kitzen sounds nice—"

"You don't get the point, Jake," Nancy inter-
jected. "I'm looking for tough, not nice."

"Oh, yeah, right," Jake muttered. "Well, then,
I'll just take down a few of these names myself."

"Jake!" Nancy cried.

"Well, if you won't go out with me anymore,"
he said with a wink, "what's a guy to do?"

Nancy shook her head laughing as Jake sauntered up to the information booth to get Jeanine's and Sara Ann's phone numbers.

Nancy quickly scribbled down the names of Mary Pearce, who liked Italian food, and Toni Scarmuzzo, who was an exchange student from, not Italy, to Nancy's surprise, but Argentina.

"One of you will be the lucky winner," she said to the cards. "Real lucky."

"Thanks again, Stephanie. I can't tell you how much I appreciate your taking Molly," Jackie said late Friday afternoon. Molly was sleeping peacefully on her mother's shoulder. "I missed you so much, Molly-pie." Jackie kissed her daughter's smooth forehead.

"No problem, Jackie," Stephanie lied. Inside, she wanted to break down and tell her how hard it had been and how Jonathan had been no help at all. If he'd only helped her once, maybe she wouldn't be so angry with him. But he hadn't.

She leaned over and kissed Molly's cheek. "I'm going to miss her. She's a wonderful baby. It's a lot of work, though. I hadn't realized." Of course, Stephanie thought, when your husband is sleeping soundly while you're playing patty-cake at 4:30 A.M. . . .

"I wish I could pay you—" Jackie began.

"Don't be silly. I wouldn't accept any money from you," Stephanie said. "We're friends."

"Okay. Well, I have to be going. If there's ever anything I can do for you . . . I know! When you and Jonathan have a baby, I'll give *you* a weekend away," Jackie offered with a smile.

"You're on," Stephanie told her. But after the last two days, she didn't think she and Jonathan would be having any children together soon. Or ever. " 'Bye, cutie!" Molly didn't stir.

"Thanks again," Jackie said.

Stephanie watched as they walked away. Molly was sweet, but Stephanie couldn't wait to take a long, hot bath and collapse into bed. She had just closed the door when it opened again and in walked Jonathan.

"Hey, Steph," he said.

Stephanie looked at him. "What were you doing, waiting outside until Jackie left with Molly? Oh, of course. You wouldn't want to have to do anything to help, like actually carry something out to her car or fill a bottle with juice—"

"Stephanie, of course I wasn't waiting outside." Jonathan walked to the refrigerator, opened it, and took out a can of soda. He cracked open the top. "Why would you say that?"

"Gee, I don't know. Maybe because it seems like such a coincidence that you'd come in two seconds after Molly left," Stephanie said.

Jonathan shrugged out of his coat and threw it across the couch. "I think I get home at almost the same time every day, Stephanie. I don't exactly plan it to the last second. And I've had it with your accusations about my not helping."

"They're not accusations," Stephanie said. "They're the truth. I just spent forty-eight hours looking after Molly, and I think you contributed—what, about one minute of help? That was when you poured cereal into a bowl."

"We've been over this, Stephanie." Jonathan sank onto the couch and clicked on the TV. "You said you'd baby-sit. You didn't ask me first. You never do."

Stephanie put her hands on her hips. "What's that supposed to mean?"

"If you'd asked me whether I wanted a baby in our apartment, I would have said no," Jonathan said. "Then you wouldn't have told Jackie yes, and you wouldn't be angry at me for not helping, when I never said I'd help in the first place. It's just like when you bought that furniture. You simply act before you think."

"Oh. So I'm dumb now, is that it?" Stephanie said, her temper rising.

"I didn't say that. But it seems as if you have a really hard time thinking about anyone but yourself," Jonathan said.

"This from a man who sat there and watched me slave away taking care of a baby without lifting a finger to help?" Stephanie scoffed. "I don't think I'm the selfish one here!"

"No, but you are the immature one," Jonathan said. "We're not playing house. We're married. We should talk about things and make decisions together. But apparently you're not ready for that, and I'm starting to think that our getting married was a big mistake."

"Starting to think? Starting to think?" Stephanie's eyes filled with angry tears. "I've been thinking that for weeks!"

She turned away, ready to march into their bedroom and slam the door. How dare Jonathan accuse her of being selfish and immature! And to say their marriage was a big mistake . . .

Wait a second, she thought. Didn't I just say the same thing? Stephanie was angry with Jonathan, but she was still in love with him. And she didn't want to lose him over an argument about a botched baby-sitting job.

She slowly turned around and looked at Jonathan. Tears were spilling down her cheeks. "I'm sorry," she said. "I didn't mean that."

Jonathan jumped off the couch and put his arms around her. "No, I'm sorry. I don't think getting married was a mistake. I was just angry, that's all." He pushed her hair back off her face and wiped the tears from her cheeks.

"Don't cry, Steph," he pleaded, tears springing to his own eyes.

"I just felt I had to help Jackie," Stephanie said. "But the pressure and everything . . . I couldn't do it all on my own."

"I'm glad you felt so generous," Jonathan said, hugging her close. "But you can't donate my time to something without asking me. Does that make sense to you?"

Stephanie nodded. "Now can we stop fighting? And never fight again?"

Joanthan laughed. "Well, I can't make you that

promise. Being married means working things out, which means you have to argue sometimes."

"Let's not call them arguments," Stephanie said, pressing her cheek to Jonathan's chest. "Let's call them discussions."

Jonathan stroked her hair. "Okay."

"I love you," Stephanie whispered, looking up at Jonathan.

"I love you, too," Jonathan said, before sealing Stephanie's lips with a deep kiss.

CHAPTER 10

"I can't believe I let you talk me into this, Nancy."
Kara stood in front of the full-length mirror in their
room. "Tim *barely* understood why I was going on
a blind date, besides which, do I even *want* to meet
this guy Michael, after everything you told me
about him?"

"Kara, we'll just see the play and maybe have coffee afterward," Nancy said. "That's it, I promise. I
just couldn't find anyone who I thought was right for
Michael, but I couldn't tell him that. And I didn't
have the heart to inflict him on someone I didn't
know—like the girls from the dating bulletin board."

"So, you thought of me." Kara rolled her eyes.
"Gee, thanks."

"Think of it this way," Nancy said. "I owe you
one."

"You bet you do," Kara replied, tugging at the scoop neck of her black dress. "Big time."

"Now, let me look at the mirror," Nancy said, trying to edge her way into the reflection.

"I'm using it," Kara said.

"Well, I need it," Nancy said, slipping her feet into a pair of chunky-heeled black shoes. "They'll be here in five minutes and I don't even know if this outfit goes together."

Kara looked over her shoulder at Nancy's fuzzy olive green sweater and short black skirt. "You look fine." Then she turned back around and started smoothing her stockings.

The telephone interrupted the battle for the mirror.

"Maybe it's Michael saying they'll be late. Better yet, maybe they're canceling," Kara said.

"Don't get too excited," Nancy said, picking up the receiver. "Hi, this is Nancy."

"Nancy, it's Stanley Trenton. Sorry to bother you on a Friday night."

Professor Trenton? "Oh, it's no bother," Nancy told him, wondering what was so urgent. "What's up?"

"Well . . . I hope this won't upset you," he began.

Nancy sat on the end of her bed. This sounded serious. "Is there news about the bomb?"

"No, it's just that I've heard that you may have a conflict of interest in investigating this story," Professor Trenton said. "I know that you're a friend of the woman who might have been the bomber's target. A very good friend."

"That's true. Bess and I have been friends for

years," Nancy said. "What does that have to do with the story?"

"Frankly, I'm worried about your objectivity," the professor said. "I don't want anything to stand in the way of our getting the best possible story. I thought I should tell you that I may have to pull you off it."

Nancy felt as if she'd just been punched in the stomach. "Pull me from the story?" she repeated. "But—"

"I know you've already put a significant amount of work into it, and I don't want to punish you for simply knowing one of the victims," Professor Trenton explained. "But my source suggested that you might be too involved to see things clearly."

Your source? Nancy thought, shook her head. You mean Michael Gianelli! The day before, she had confided in him that it was hard working on a story while she was so concerned about Bess. He'd turned it into Nancy's being *unable* to work on the story.

"Professor Trenton, I think you may have gotten the wrong impression," Nancy said. "My relationship with Bess Marvin does not affect my judgment or my performance. If anything, it sharpens them. I want to find out who the bomber is, just like everyone else. You don't doubt that, do you?"

"Nancy, we haven't worked together as a team very long. I don't really know what to think," Professor Trenton said. "All I know is that this concerns me."

"Please don't pull me from the story," Nancy said.

"I won't do it unless I have a good reason," Professor Trenton said. "I am sorry, Nancy. Good night."

Nancy hung up the phone just as a knock sounded on the suite door.

"That's them," Kara predicted.

"I hope so," Nancy muttered. She no longer cared what her outfit looked like. When she got to the door, she yanked it open. "You're such a jerk!" she cried out.

Gus smiled nervously. "Hi, you must be Nancy Drew."

"How could you do that to me?" Nancy demanded of the figure behind Gus.

"I'm Gus Lindgren. Pleased to meet you." Gus stepped inside to get out of the line of fire.

"Me? What did I do?" Michael asked.

"Don't give me that! I was starting to think we could work together. I thought maybe you were decent after all." Nancy threw up her hands. "I confided in you. And you used that information to muscle me out of the way so you could grab the bomb story for yourself. Well, you won't get away with it."

"Nancy, Nancy . . ." Michael raised his hands in a gesture of having nothing to hide. "What are you talking about?"

"Professor Trenton just called me. He's questioning my credibility because *you* told him I was Bess's friend." Nancy was seething.

"I may have mentioned it, but I never made a big deal out of it," Michael said with a shrug. "I mean, if we do stories about campus events, we're going to know people. That goes with the territory. Doesn't he understand that?"

"*He's* not the problem. You are," Nancy said.

"I'll talk to him, okay?" Michael suggested. "Tonight let's just try to have fun. May I come in?"

Fun? When he was sabotaging her journalism career before it had scarcely started? Good thing I'm his friend's date, Nancy thought. If Michael were my date, he wouldn't survive the night.

"See? I told you this would be fun!" Nikki smiled as she took off her coat. She tossed it into a pile that had already accumulated on the couch just inside the door of the Beta house.

"I think I'll keep my jacket on," Montana said.

"Montana! You can't hide in your jacket any more than you could hide under that ugly straw hat," Nikki said. "You have to face your fears. C'mon, loosen up, chill out."

"It's my favorite leather jacket, okay? I don't want anyone to steal it, that's all," Montana said.

"Oh." Nikki gave her a questioning look. "You're not getting all self-conscious on me again, are you?"

"No. Ray and Cory would never show up at a Beta party, unless they were performing," Montana said. "I'm safe here."

Two guys approached them, wearing football helmets with a bowl of chips glued to the top of one, and a bowl of onion dip glued to the other. "Did I say safe?" Montana asked Nikki.

"Care for a snack?" The tall guys crouched down, so that Nikki and Montana could reach the bowls.

"You guys spent a lot of time on this idea, didn't you?" Montana said, dragging a chip through the dip.

"Anything for a party!" They disappeared into the crowded main party room.

"Whatever," Nikki said. "Come on, let's see who's here."

They were halfway to the dance floor when Montana got cut off by a roving crowd of Betas.

"Excuse me," she said. "Coming through. Hot coffee. Excuse me."

Just as she had pushed her way through, she heard a voice.

"That's a really cool jacket."

"Thanks, I got it in—" Montana said before she realized who she was talking to. "Cory," she muttered. "Excuse me."

"Don't go away yet." Cory caught the sleeve of her jacket. "Unless of course you're going out there to dance with me."

"Actually, I was going to dance with Nikki," Montana told him, feeling her face start to blush. Why was he being nice to her when he had seen what an idiot she was?

She practically ran onto the dance floor, almost knocking Nikki over. "Don't do that again," she yelled into her friend's ear. "You stranded me with Cory!"

"Sorry! What did he say?" Nikki asked.

"He said he liked my jacket," Montana said, rolling her eyes. "Isn't that dumb?"

"Complimenting you is dumb?" Nikki asked.

"He only said that because he feels sorry for me. He thinks I'm pathetic!" Montana cried.

"Or maybe he just liked your jacket!" Nikki yelled.

Montana shook her head. "No, he thinks it's sad that I like Ray and Ray doesn't like me. He thinks I'm a loser. Come on, let's move over there. I don't want him looking at me and feeling sorry for me all night."

"I'm sure he has better things to do," Nikki commented as she glanced across the crowded dance floor at Cory. "Forget it, Montana. He's not looking at you. See?"

But when Montana got up the nerve to look in Cory's direction, he was staring right at her.

Bess stood center stage, clutching Brian's hand as they took a bow with the full cast. Her eyes filled with tears as she and Brian stepped forward to take their own bow. They were happy tears, proud tears.

The curtain came down, and Brian hugged Bess tightly. "We did it, girl!"

"We were awesome," Bess told him.

"Yeah, weren't we?" Brian smiled and gave Bess a big kiss. For once, she'd said "we," instead of saying Brian alone was great. He couldn't have wished for more.

Backstage, the director, Jeanne Glasseburg, hugged Bess, then Brian. "I knew you could do it, Bess. Brian, you were masterful. Let's keep it up for tomorrow night."

"Great job, Bess," Justin said as they walked past him on their way to the dressing rooms. "Uh, you, too, Brian."

"Thanks, Justin," Bess replied. "You're the best."

"At least it wasn't a bomb!" Brian said, very pleased with his pun. Justin looked horrified.

"Don't listen to him," Bess said as she pushed her costar along.

Outside of the dressing rooms, Brian and Bess congratulated each other once more.

"See you at the Cave to celebrate," Brian reminded Bess.

"I'll be there after I find Nancy and George. They said they'd wait in the lobby," Bess said. She pushed the door open to the crowded women's dressing room and entered to a round of applause from her fellow female actors.

Bess realized she was exhausted when she had trouble opening her locker. The door must be jammed, she thought. Bess finally felt it give. The door swung open and a bouquet of roses fell into her hands.

Everyone around her oohed and aahed, which increased Bess's fluttery feeling of romance. After dressing—she didn't bother removing her makeup—

Bess tore out of the dressing room to meet George and Nancy. On the way she stopped to show Marisa the flowers.

"From who?" Marisa asked after admiring them.

"My secret admirer!" Bess answered. "It's a long story. I'll tell you about it tomorrow! Gotta run."

When Bess arrived in the lobby, George had to pull Nancy away from an argument with Michael to greet her.

"You did great!" George said, hugging her cousin.

Nancy wrapped an arm around Bess's shoulders. "Fantastic, Bess!"

"Who are these from?" George asked, sticking her nose in Bess's bouquet. "Your secret admirer?"

"Don't tell us they're from your parents or Brian," Nancy warned.

Bess beamed and read them the card. " 'You were wonderful tonight. Getting curious? If you want to know who I am, meet me at the Clock Tower, Saturday at noon.' "

"What do you guys think? Should I meet him?" Bess asked. The idea was both thrilling and frightening. If the guy was as nice as he seemed, it would be fun. But if he was some kind of crazy . . .

"I don't know. He might be for real. Or it might be a trap," Nancy said.

"A trap? You mean, by the same person who set off the bomb?" George asked.

Nancy nodded. "It might not be safe to meet whoever this is by yourself, Bess. If you want to go, maybe you should show this note to the police, or campus security."

"Good idea," Bess said. "But if it's really my secret admirer, and he turns out to be a great guy— I hope I don't scare him off."

"You'll have to take that risk," Nancy told her. "I don't want to sound dramatic, but you could be putting your life in danger. As far as we know, this person could be a total stranger."

"I'll go with you, Bess," George offered. "And we'll get security to check the area in and around the Clock Tower first."

"We'll ask for a photo ID," Bess began. "Then we'll ask him to walk through a metal detector, take his fingerprints, check his DNA . . ."

"I know it doesn't sound very romantic," Nancy told her. "But you have to be careful, Bess. You never know."

"You're right," Bess agreed. "And if all the security doesn't scare him off, he's bound to be worth the trouble."

Bess had just one wish in her heart: Please, oh, please, don't be the bomber!

CHAPTER 11

As Nancy walked back to join Kara, Michael, and Gus, she caught a glimpse of Daphne through the open door to the theater. She stood alone below the stage, gazing up at the drawn curtains. Nancy had to admit that the sight caused her a pang of compassion.

Nancy began to wonder whether she'd been wrong about suspecting Daphne of planting the bomb to get rid of Bess. After all, wouldn't she have tried again before opening night when the bomb failed? Opening night was over. Bess was a hit. It was too late for Daphne. Bess's secret admirer suddenly became a more likely suspect. Who was he? He'd sent Bess flowers to introduce himself, but had he also set off the bomb to get her attention?

"There's a party at Beta tonight. Actually, my boyfriend's there already," Kara was saying to Gus as Nancy walked up to her. She glanced at her watch. "Would you mind if we met him there?"

"Sounds great," Gus said. "Just promise me you'll introduce me to some of your single female friends when we get there."

"Definitely," Kara said, slapping him on the back as if they were long-lost buddies. "Have you ever listened to my radio show? I have two lovely co-hosts, and neither one is dating anyone right now."

"Wait a second," Nancy said. "You guys aren't leaving, are you?"

"Hmm, let's see—we could sit here and continue to listen to you guys argue all night," Gus said, "or we could go to a raging, all-night party and have fun. What do you think, Kara? What should we do?" He bit his lip, as if it were an agonizing decision.

Kara laughed. "See you later, Nancy. Why don't the two of you stop by the Beta house when you've finished arguing—if you ever finish arguing."

Nancy watched Kara and Gus walk out the door and into the night. How could her roommate abandon her like that? Kara was supposed to be Michael's date for the night. Now she was stuck with him.

Michael was tapping his foot against the carpet. "So. What do we do now?" he asked.

"I guess we have to admit something," Nancy said, sitting on one of the plush velveteen benches in the lobby.

"And what's that?" Michael said, sitting beside her.

"That we're lousy at picking out dates for each other," Nancy said.

"At least I set you up with someone who wasn't already taken," Michael said.

Nancy felt a small smile curl up at the corners of her mouth. "That was kind of lame, wasn't it? But did you honestly think I'd have anything in common with Gus?"

"What's wrong with Gus?" Michael sounded offended. "He's a nice guy."

"For a gym buddy, maybe."

"Hey, I work out with him all the time," Michael said.

"Precisely, but do you hang out with him discussing current events over cappuccino?" Nancy asked.

"No, but—" Michael began to defend his pal.

"Case closed," Nancy said definitively.

"Well, we at least could've had a good time if you hadn't been so mad at me when we first showed up. You set the tone for the whole night."

Nancy's eyes widened. "Are you saying it's *my* fault everyone had a rotten time? Because I'm not the one who told Professor Trenton I should be taken off our top story. You're the one whose petty jealousy is responsible for ruining this whole evening."

"I'm jealous? Right," Michael scoffed. "Nancy, I didn't mean for Professor Trenton to take you off the story. I only meant—"

"That you'd rather cover the story all on your own. Well, bravo, Michael, bravo. Nice solo performance." Nancy clapped her hands.

"You know . . . I can't remember having a worse night," Michael said.

"Neither can I," Nancy said.

Silence descended as the two sat fuming side by side.

"Hey, folks, we're closing up." A student usher held the door open for Nancy and Michael and then locked it behind them. They stood for a minute on the steps of the theater.

"Look, do you want to at least drop by the Beta party?" Michael asked.

Nancy shrugged. "Sure. Just don't tell anyone we came together."

"Hey, don't worry about it. I have a reputation to protect," Michael said.

"Here you are." Stephanie set down a large slice of chocolate cake with chocolate frosting in front of Jonathan.

"Did you bake this? For me?" Jonathan asked. He leaned toward her, giving her a quick kiss.

"No, but I did pick it out at the bakery just for you," Stephanie told him, sitting down on the couch next to him late Friday night.

"Same difference," Jonathan said, laughing. "Thanks." He dug in and grinned like a true chocoholic. "You've really been making an effort tonight, and I want you to know that I appreciate it. I appreciate *you.*"

"You should," Stephanie said, lifting a forkful of cake to her lips. "Because I'm crazy about you. And I'm not going to stop spoiling you." Not until she could get the memory of their fight that afternoon out of her head. It was too scary to think about.

"Well, you might have to," Jonathan said. "Just for a little while."

"Why?" Stephanie asked. "So you can devote all your time to *me?* Hey, I like the sound of this."

"I would love to devote all my time to you. But right now I can't. I just found out that I need to go out of town next Thursday, and I'll be gone almost a whole week. It's a management training program in Chicago," Jonathan explained. "I'm one of the three people at Berrigan's who was chosen to go."

"Congratulations, honey! That's great," Stephanie said. "Does this mean you might get a promotion soon?"

"Probably," Jonathan said. "But what it definitely means is that I'll be out of town for a week, maybe a weekend, too. I'm sorry."

"What are you sorry about?" Stephanie asked. "You have to go."

"I know, but things were sort of rocky between us this week, and I don't want you to think I'm doing this on purpose," Jonathan said.

"I wouldn't think that," Stephanie said. "It's your job. Anyway, maybe spending some time apart will be good for us."

"Don't even say that, Steph," Jonathan protested. "I'm going to miss you so much."

"And I'll miss you, too. Horribly." Stephanie smiled at him. "But you have to do what you have to do."

"I hate leaving you here, all by yourself," Jonathan said. "Won't you be lonely?"

All of a sudden, Stephanie remembered leaning against her old closet at Thayer the other day. She remembered how much she had missed the suite and how much fun it had been to drop in on everyone. Wouldn't it be great to go out to a bunch of campus parties and stay out all night rather than have to go home at the same time Jonathan did? "Well, maybe I won't stay here while you're gone," Stephanie said slowly.

"I'm sorry, hon, I already asked if you could come with me," Jonathan said. "But—"

"I'm not talking about that," Stephanie said a little impatiently. "I was just thinking that since Nadia's gone, Casey doesn't have a roommate."

Jonathan looked at her blankly.

"I bet if I asked, I could stay in my old room while you're gone," Stephanie explained. "Isn't it perfect? I won't be lonely, and you'll know that I'm okay."

"You really want to spend the week in a dorm?" Jonathan asked. "That doesn't sound like much fun, though I would feel better knowing you're not alone," Jonathan said. "I still hate to leave you for a week."

"I know." Stephanie snuggled up to her husband.

"But look at it this way. We'll have a great welcome home party." She picked up a piece of cake on Jonathan's fork and put it to his lips. "Cake and all."

George made a production of opening the Saturday morning Weston newspaper while standing in the cafeteria line for brunch. "It says here, and I quote, 'The clear star of Wilder's latest student production is Bess Marvin, a freshman in the drama department and one of the most promising actors to hit Weston in a long time. Don't miss *Cat on a Hot Tin Roof,* playing Saturday night and next weekend as well.' "

"I hope Daphne doesn't see that glowing review about you," Nancy said, putting a glass of orange juice on her tray.

"I'm sure she's already seen it," Bess said. "None of us went to bed until the paper hit the newsstands. She's probably writing a letter of complaint to the editor at this very moment."

"If she's read it, we'd better have someone taste your food before you eat it, Bess," said Marisa, who had joined them at Bess's invitation. "It may be poisoned."

Bess laughed. "Hey, read what it says about Brian."

"Let me see." George skimmed the article. " 'The chemistry between Brick and Maggie is near perfect. Brian Daglian turns in an inspired performance as Brick and shows he has the range to tackle any role.' "

"Oh, good!" Nancy said. "He'll be thrilled."

Marisa turned to Bess. "So, what are we having for brunch?"

"Hmm. How about a dozen omelets, a mountain of toast, and a billion cinnamon rolls," Bess joked. "No?"

"Sounds good, but I think I'll stick to a fruit salad and cereal," Marisa said. "Thanks for asking me to brunch with your friends. I just knew when I woke up this morning that this was going to be one of *those* days." She made a face. "One step forward—"

"Two steps forward, if you please," Bess said, nudging Marisa's tray along. "You're doing great. Just keep telling yourself that, because it's true." They followed George and Nancy to a large, round table near the window.

"I want to know when the police are going to do something about Daphne—or whoever—setting off that pipe bomb," Marisa said as they sat down.

"Actually, I'm not sure that Daphne did do it," Nancy said to everyone's surprise. "There's someone a little higher up on my list."

"Really?" Bess raised her eyebrows, and then it dawned on her. "Oh, not my secret admirer, Nancy." Her enthusiasm about meeting him suddenly disappeared.

"I'm sorry, Bess," Nancy said. "But all we know about him is that he's been acting very secretively and that he sends flowers."

"Any idea who he is?" Marisa tore a piece of wheat toast in half and took a bite.

"Actually, something weird occurred to me last night—this morning—when I got back to my room after the reviews came out," Bess said. She turned to George, who seemed absorbed in removing the raisins from a muffin. "Remember when you came over the other morning, and those daisies were in the hall?"

"Yes," George said. "You were on the phone when I got there, with what's-his-name."

"Who's what's-his-name?" Nancy asked.

"Justin. He called to check on me. And we were talking. Only, I think he was about to ask me out, when George showed up. I guess I cut him off," Bess explained. "I told him about the daisies and he got all nervous. Maybe he sent the flowers and was calling to find out if I got them, but was too shy to say so. He could be my secret admirer."

"I don't think so," Marisa said, shaking her head.

"Why not? Is he dating someone else?" George asked.

"I don't think so," Marisa said. "But, Bess, when you came backstage last night to show me your roses, he was there watching. He looked furious when you said they were from a secret admirer."

"Furious—as in he was jealous?" Nancy asked.

"Looked like it to me," Marisa said. "He stormed off, and I didn't see him for the rest of the night. If he *had* sent you the roses, then he would have been thrilled to see you so happy about getting them. So I think it has to be someone else."

"But Justin did seem really interested in you, when I talked to him about the bombing," Nancy said to Bess. "Almost as though he was thrilled to have had the chance to save your life. Like you were a celebrity or something."

"Maybe he just knows talent when he sees it." Bess alone laughed at her joke. She didn't know why, but the idea of Justin liking her so much made her uncomfortable. She hated having to tell a guy who liked her that she wasn't interested in him.

"So Justin likes you, but he's not your secret admirer," Nancy mused. "Interesting."

"More like annoying," George said. "Don't you have any clue who this secret admirer guy is?"

"I, for one, can't wait to find out who he is. As long as he's not dangerous," Marisa announced.

"But it's a very real possibility that he is," Nancy said. "Look, you guys be careful today when you go to meet him at the Clock Tower. Sorry, but right now I have to run. I just thought of something that I need to check out." She pushed back her chair and stood up.

"What is it?" Bess asked.

"It's Justin," Nancy said. "I need to talk to him again."

"Nancy, Justin is the quietest, most mild-mannered guy in the world. I can't imagine him swatting a fly." Bess couldn't let Nancy leave thinking Justin was crazy.

"You didn't see the look on his face last night," Marisa said.

Nancy phoned Michael from the phone in the cafeteria. "You have reached the Gianelli residence, but we are not available to answer your call right now. Please leave a message. If this is an emergency for Lawrence Gianelli, please hang up and dial 555-4324." Nancy recognized Michael's voice, but she had never heard of Lawrence Gianelli before. That's probably his dad, she thought. He must be a doctor or something.

"Michael," she began, "it seems that Justin, the lighting director, may be the one we're looking for. I thought I'd see if you wanted to go with me to talk to him, but as you're not home, I'll—" Nancy stopped suddenly. Outside the lobby window she spied Michael walking across the quad with a police officer. "Forget it," she finished, and hung up the phone. She ran out the door and yelled Michael's name, but the men were too far away to hear her.

That's got to be his source! Nancy thought as she started jogging in their direction. She caught up to them just outside of Java Joe's.

"Gianelli, wait up," she called out breathlessly.

When the two men turned around, Nancy couldn't believe her eyes. Was she in the Twilight Zone? There stood the Michael she knew, and next to him stood a middle-aged Michael: same height, same build, same eyes, and the same hair, though the older man was graying.

In an instant, one and one added up to two: Michael's source was his father! Lawrence Gianelli was a cop. So much for Michael's "simple, standard journalistic practice" to get information from the police. They probably talked about cases over breakfast.

"Hey, Michael. Got a second?" Nancy didn't wait for an answer but turned to the uniformed officer. "Hi, I'm Nancy Drew." She held out her hand to Michael's father.

"Sergeant Lawrence Gianelli." He smiled at Nancy and shook her hand. "Nice to meet you. You two in the same class or something?"

"Kind of," Michael said, looking very uncomfortable. "We're doing that TV show together." Nancy caught a vague look of panic on Michael's face.

"Forgive me for interrupting," Nancy said politely. "You were probably going over some important case detail—"

"Actually, we were talking about what to get his brother for a wedding present," Sergeant Gianelli said.

"Oh, a high-security case." Nancy gave Michael a meaningful glance. "Well, do you have a second to discuss the bombing? Because I have a new idea about who might be behind it."

"I'd love to hear what you think," Michael's father said. "We were just going in for a cup of coffee. Care to join us?"

"Thank you," Nancy said, smiling at Michael's obvious discomfort. "I'd love that."

Unlike his son, Lawrence Gianelli had the manners of a gentleman. He offered to buy Nancy's coffee and placed her order for her after asking what she'd like.

As they sat down, Nancy picked up the conversation where they'd left off outside. "Let me back up. You remember Bess, the lead in the play?"

Nancy asked. Both men nodded. "Well, she has a secret admirer, who I thought might be Justin Beckett. He seemed so attached to her and protective."

"Who's Justin?" Sergeant Gianelli asked.

"He's the lighting director for the play. But now I've changed my thinking because when he saw her get roses from her secret admirer last night, he became furious," Nancy explained.

"So he *does* have a thing for Bess, but he's not the secret admirer?" Michael asked.

Nancy turned to him. "Remember Justin's excitement when he told us how he had saved her life? I think he could have planted the bomb so that he *could* save her."

Michael acted skeptical. "That's crazy!"

"No, it's not. It makes a certain kind of sense," Nancy argued.

"Right. Whenever I like a girl, I always push her in front of a speeding car, so I can grab her out of the way before she gets hit," Michael snorted.

"I hope not. That would mean you're a sociopath. Which, if I'm right, is what Justin is," Nancy retorted.

"Come on, do you expect me to believe—"

"She's right, Mike." The sergeant not only cut Michael off, he called him Mike. Nancy was having a field day. "It's not unheard of. I can remember a case a few years ago in which a man was so obsessed with a woman that he attacked her viciously enough that she passed out. Then he rescued her. He wore a mask to hide the identity of the attacker but took it off to play the hero."

"Yeah, but that guy was seriously bad news," Michael said. "Justin is so mild-mannered. He's a study geek, Dad. He's skinny and short—"

"So? That doesn't mean anything," his father said. "Or did you think there was a height requirement for criminal activity?"

Nancy thoroughly enjoyed watching someone else give Michael a hard time for a change.

"Thank you, Sergeant Gianelli," she said. "It's worth talking to Justin, don't you think? We don't have any other leads right now."

"Besides Daphne," Michael reminded her.

"I've written her off," Nancy explained. "If Daphne was serious about getting Bess's part in the play, she would have kept trying until she either succeeded or got caught. She didn't."

"Should we go find Justin?" Michael asked.

Nancy couldn't tell if he was asking her, or his father. "Yes," they both answered at once.

"And tell me if you find out anything I should know," Michael's father added. "I've got to run. I can't believe I'm using my college kid as a source." He shook his head.

As Sergeant Gianelli walked out of the coffeehouse, Nancy turned to Michael. "And I can't believe you're using your dad as a source."

"Hey, a source is a source," Michael said. "Who cares how you get one?"

"It's just that some people wouldn't be ashamed

to admit that their father was a cop, Michael," Nancy said. That shut him up.

They silently put on their coats and headed out. Neither one said another word until they were just outside Justin's dorm.

"*Ssst,* Nancy," Michael whispered hoarsely. He grabbed her arm and pulled her behind an evergreen bush.

"Hey—" Nancy began to cry out, but Michael silenced her with his hand over her mouth.

"It's Justin and Max. They're in the parking lot. I don't think they saw us," Michael said.

"Why don't we just go talk to them?" Nancy asked.

"From what I saw, I don't think we should interrupt them," Michael said.

"What do you mean?" Nancy had just about had enough of Michael's pushing her around.

"Let's get closer to them," Michael said. "Follow me."

The two managed to squeeze their way between the bushes and the wall of the dorm to get closer to the parking lot unseen. As they got closer, they could pick up some words and phrases, but nothing coherent. Suddenly Justin's voice rang out.

"Just stay away from her, Max!"

Then Nancy heard the sickening sound of a fist being delivered to a man's solar plexus. "I'm serious," Justin declared as Max fell to the ground. "Remember that."

Nancy and Michael instantly started pushing their way through the scratchy evergreen boughs, but before they could break clear of the growth, they heard a car door slam, an engine kick in, and tires squeal away.

Max lay on the asphalt gulping for air.

"You'll be all right," Michael said as he knelt down and helped Max to a seated position. "Just take as many deep breaths as you can."

A couple minutes later Max was able to talk.

"He's a lunatic!" he said. He started to stand, his hand cradling his midriff. "Oof!" he exclaimed.

"Take it easy, Max," Nancy said.

"Hey, do I know you?" he asked.

Nancy introduced herself first. "I'm Nancy Drew, a friend of Bess Marvin's. And this is Michael Gianelli. We're looking into the pipe bomb explosion for a television news story."

Max suddenly seemed to get a little nervous.

"Can you tell us what just went on here?" Michael asked.

"No," Max said. "It was a personal thing. And besides, I have to go." He checked his watch. "Oh, great!" he muttered. "I'll be late."

"Please, couldn't we talk for just a few minutes?" Nancy asked. "It could help us find out the identity of the bomber."

"Sorry, you're on your own there. All I can tell you is that it's not me," Max said. Then he turned around and sprinted off.

Nancy turned back to Michael. "He wasn't very helpful."

"Makes me a little suspicious," Michael said.

"But since we don't seem to have anyone out here to talk to—"

"We might as well check out Justin's room—before he gets back." Nancy finished his sentence for him.

"Thank you," Michael said. "I think I could have gotten the words out myself."

"Oh, come off it, Michael! Let's just go up to Justin's room—okay?" Nancy snapped.

"Are you suggesting—" Michael said with a leer.

"I'm suggesting that if Justin is psycho enough to plant a bomb for the woman he loves, I'd hate to think what he'd do to us if we were still in his room when he came back."

CHAPTER 12

It's noon. He isn't here," Bess complained. "I'm leaving."

"Chill out," George said. "Give him a chance to make it up the hill."

"If he's really my secret admirer and not the bomber, he should be here," Bess said. "Unless he chickened out or got scared off by the police." Campus security had spent a half hour searching the clearing and wooded area around the Clock Tower. Two officers were stationed inside, in case the situation got dangerous.

"Or maybe he saw that I brought a friend, and he didn't like that," Bess said, worried.

"Hey, if he doesn't like me, then there's no way he can go out with you," George declared. "Wait, isn't that someone walking up the hill?"

Bess stood on her tiptoes. "Yes, but I can't see who it is." Something about the guy looked familiar, however.

"He's carrying a red rose. That's so sweet!" George commented.

"It's not Justin, is it?" Bess asked nervously.

George shook her head. "No. He's taller than Justin. With really short blond hair."

"Max?" Bess suddenly cried as he got closer. "It's you?"

"Who's Max?" George demanded.

"He works in the sound booth, for the play," Bess said, walking forward to meet him.

"He should be *in* the play," George murmured, following Bess. "And in the movies and in magazines . . ."

"Hi, Bess, it's me," Max said, holding the long-stemmed rose out to her. "And this is for you, if you want it."

Bess took the rose and held it to her nose, inhaling deeply. "It's wonderful, Max. Thanks. Why wouldn't I want a rose from you?"

"I don't know who you were expecting," Max said shyly. "Maybe you're disappointed?"

"Not at all!" Bess said. "Surprised, maybe. I didn't think my secret admirer was someone from the play." She turned around. "This is my cousin George. She came along in case you turned out to be the bo—a creep."

"Hi. Nice to meet you, Max," George said. She tugged on Bess's sleeve. "Do you want me to go?"

Bess didn't know what to say. She thought she

trusted Max, but as Nancy had said, she had to be careful. "Not yet," Bess told her. She turned to Max. "I hope you won't think this is weird, but I asked campus security to check out the area and stick around while we talked. Because of the bomb." She waved at the two uniformed officers who were standing in the doorway of the Clock Tower. They nodded but made no move to leave.

"I understand," Max said. "That was a crazy scene the other night. Who could blame you for being careful?" He shook his head. "I wish the police would catch whoever did it. I don't feel it's safe around the theater."

"I know. Neither do I," Bess said.

"I've got an idea," George said. "Why don't we walk over to the Cave? We can talk a little on the way, and then you guys can spend some time alone, but in a public place."

"Sounds like a plan," Max said. "If it's okay with you, Bess. Or if you want to hang here with the security guards, that's okay, too."

How can I not trust such a thoughtful guy? Bess wondered. "Come on, let's go!"

"Your credit card or mine?" Michael asked, reaching for his wallet.

"Yours, if you're good at it," Nancy said.

"Hey. My dad taught me all the tricks of hardened criminals," Michael said. He slid the card into the door's crack and jiggled it up and down, pressing on the handle. There was a click, and the door swung open. "Presto," he said softly.

"Thanks." Nancy stepped into the small, single dorm room. Justin had covered the walls with theater posters. His desk was overflowing with papers, including the reviews of last night's performance. Nancy spied something familiar half hidden under the tousled sheets of Justin's bed and went to check it out while Michael poked around the desk.

"Michael? Look at this." Nancy held up a small wooden box, identical to the one in Daphne's bag. "Dragon Manufacturing."

"So either he found the second box backstage, like Daphne—"

"Which means that an awful lot of cast and crew members go through the trash every night," Nancy cut in. "Highly unlikely."

"Or Justin used the first box and kept the second box for later," Michael finished.

Nancy opened the box. "Only later is right now. Michael, the box is empty."

"Unless he used all the firecrackers for the first bomb—but he couldn't have. That bomb was too small—*uh-oh*," Michael exclaimed.

Nancy walked over to the desk to look at what Michael had found. He was looking down at Justin's wastebasket. On top of the trash and littered on the floor were crumpled and torn pieces of paper with writing on them and firecracker wrappers.

Nancy picked up one of the scraps of paper. " 'Dear Bess,' " she read out loud. " 'I love you so much I can't stand not to be near to you. I can't let you go out with anyone else. Please understand.' "

She threw the paper aside, her heart pounding

in her throat. She felt as if she was going to be sick to her stomach. Meanwhile, Michael read aloud another: " 'Bess, my life is nothing without you. Say you'll be mine forever. If you don't—' " The note broke off there. "Come on, Nancy—we've got to find Bess," Michael said.

Nancy steadied herself. Justin was obsessed with Bess, and he was probably carrying a bomb around with him, looking for her. "How does he think he'll win her love?" she whispered. "By killing her?"

"He's not thinking," Michael said, taking Nancy's hand and pulling her out of the room. "He's crazy. But we can still stop him, okay?"

Nancy nodded as she followed Michael down the hall.

"Some friends." Montana marched up the stairs to the radio station's recording studio, stomping her feet on each step. All she had asked for was a little help. Just this once, would Nikki and Kara take charge, and let her stay in the background.

But no. At the last minute they'd backed out of hosting the show featuring Radical Moves. They had said something about the flu. As if she hadn't heard that one before. Now she had to interview Ray and Cory by herself, every second wishing she could crawl into her headphones and stay there forever.

She walked into the studio and took off her coat. Joseph Sanchez was wrapping up his Saturday jazz and blues program. She glanced at the clock on the wall. Only four minutes before she died of utter humiliation.

"How's it going, Montana?" Joseph asked, taking off his headphones as he started playing his final selection for the day.

"Not great. Can I just say that? Not good at all." Montana settled into a chair in the control booth. "In fact, I think I'd rather be doing anything else right now."

"Reconsidering your radio career?" Joseph asked.

"Reconsidering my college career."

There was a quiet knock on the door, and Cory poked his head through the opening. "Okay if I come in?"

"I'm all done here. Have my seat," Joseph offered, getting to his feet. "You guys were great the other night. Maybe you should think about moving more in a blues direction."

Montana kept herself busy fiddling with the control board and setting up an extra mike so she wouldn't have to look at Cory. *I could write a great blues song,* she thought. *Call it "Stuck in the Radio Studio with the Man Who Don't Love Me Blues."*

"We'll work on it," Cory told Joseph as Joseph walked out. "Hey, Montana," he said.

She nodded briefly at him and focused on getting ready for air time. *Nice of Ray to show up on time,* Montana thought. *Maybe he's as embarrassed as I am, if that's humanly possible.* "You can talk into this mike here, okay? You might want to slide that chair over," Montana told Cory.

"Okay. No problem," Cory said. "Thanks again for having us on the show. You don't have to, you know."

"Good afternoon, everyone, and welcome to 'Wild About Wilder,'" Montana said into the microphone with a pointed look at Cory. "We're here today with Radical Moves, one of the area's most exciting new bands. We'll take your calls later, but first a little music."

The studio door began to open as Montana played Radical Moves's demo tape. She glanced up nervously, expecting Ray to slouch into the room. But it wasn't Ray. It was a male student Montana didn't recognize.

"We're on the air," Cory told him in a whisper. "Maybe you could come back—"

"I'm not going anywhere," he said, his voice trembling. He opened up his backpack and lifted out a large package. It looked like several sticks wrapped together.

"What's that?" Montana asked.

"It's a bomb, Montana Smith. I could blow this whole place apart," the student threatened.

Montana's heart started beating faster. She knew suddenly what it was like to feel faint. So this was the Hewlitt bomber.

"Why would you want to do that?" Cory asked. "Come on, man—"

"Shut up! I'm in control now." The guy took a lighter out of his pocket and set it and the bomb on the table. "I'll set this bomb off right now, unless you do *exactly* what I say."

"Please, please don't hurt us," Montana begged. "Just tell us what you want."

"I want to go on the air. Now," he demanded. "Give me the microphone!"

"Your friend's nice," Max said after George left him and Bess at a table in the middle of the crowded Cave. "No, wait—she's your cousin."

"George is both friend and cousin," Bess said. She took a sip of her mineral water. "It's really nice to have family around. We're lucky we've always gotten along."

"You're not kidding," Max said. "I have a lot of cousins, but I'm not close to them. I guess it's because we live so far apart."

"What about brothers or sisters?"

"I have an older sister, who's in law school, and a younger brother in high school," Max said. "Typical nuclear all-American family." He smiled. "We're actually incredibly boring."

"No way!" Bess said. "Anyone who works in theater is fundamentally interesting. At least to me."

"And to themselves." Max grinned. "Especially if your name is Daphne Gillman."

"Ugh." Bess groaned. "Don't remind me. I'm feeling ill enough as it is." She paused, wondering whether to tell Max anything about her problems lately.

"You're not feeling well?" Max asked. "I'm sorry, Bess—do you want to go?"

"No, I don't. What I was trying to say was . . .

it's kind of hard for me to hang out here," Bess said.

"Really? How come?" Max asked, sipping a chocolate milkshake.

"Maybe I shouldn't tell you all this." Bess fiddled with the napkin dispenser on the table.

"Bess, I want to get to know you," Max said. "I already like you, so don't worry about what I might think."

"Really?" Bess asked, wrinkling her nose.

"Really. Tell me," Max urged. "What is it about the Cave that bugs you? The constant smell of greasy fries and burned coffee or the fact that the tables have this sticky feeling, like somebody spilled maple syrup twenty years ago and it never quite came off?"

Bess laughed. "Yeah, that pretty much covers it. You see, I have a problem with food. I suffered from bulimia not too long ago and I'm still learning to deal with it."

"You have bulimia?" Max asked. "Wow. I would never have guessed."

"You know about it?" Bess was surprised.

"Sure. My sister went through a period where she was bulimic," Max said. "It lasted for about a year. I think it was her first year in college. Yeah, it was."

"You know, I started a support group recently, for other people with eating disorders," Bess told him. "And more than half were freshmen."

"I guess for some people it's hard to move away

from home," Max said. "Things can seem so out of control. So, do you feel comfortable with it now?"

"Pretty comfortable, but I'm not all the way there yet," Bess admitted. "I still have some rough moments. I should tell you—what brought it on was when my boyfriend, Paul, was killed in a motorcycle crash."

Max looked taken aback. "When did that happen?"

"A couple of months ago," Bess said. "It was horrible."

"I bet," Max said sympathetically. "I'm sorry, Bess. That must have been hard."

"It was. And I didn't handle it well at all," Bess said.

"Hey, there's no right or wrong way to handle something like that," Max said. "Don't beat yourself up. You did the best you could."

"Thanks for saying that. You're right, I know. I just forget I know sometimes. For a long time, I refused to deal with it," Bess said. "I kept going around like everything was fine, until food became the outlet for my feelings."

"So basically, you've had a really great freshman year." Max smiled. "I'm sorry it's been rough. Losing your boyfriend must have been incredibly painful. But you seem to be doing well now, Bess. You really do."

"So you don't think I'm a basket case, after everything I just told you?" Bess asked.

"No." Max laughed. "Bess, I think you're great. I mean, here you are, you're still mourning the loss of your boyfriend, starring in *Cat on a Hot Tin*

Roof, dealing with bulimia, now the bomb and all. It would be really easy just to drop out of Wilder, move home, and pretend none of this ever happened. Or stay in bed for six months."

"I tried that," Bess said. "After six days it gets really boring." She smiled. "Actually, six hours was enough."

"Yeah, you've got a lot of energy. It's hard to picture you sitting around doing nothing," Max said.

"Actually, I'm good at that. Especially when I have a lot of homework due," Bess joked.

"It's a busy time," Max began. "But would you like to get together next weekend, go out or something?"

Bess couldn't believe this terrific guy! She had thought that any guy she met now would think she had too much emotional baggage. But Max seemed to think her life was perfectly normal, considering the circumstances.

"I'd love to go out again," Bess said. "Maybe we could go to Club Z Saturday, after the cast party. Do you like—"

"Bess! George told me you guys were here. Sorry to interrupt, but you have to come with us right now," Nancy said, rushing into the Cave and picking up Bess's coat and purse.

"What's going on?" Bess asked, confused. What was Nancy saying? And why was Michael with her?

"Justin has a bomb. He's holding Cory and Montana hostage at the radio station," Michael said. "And he wants to talk to you."

"Justin's the bomber?" Max stared at Bess.

"I can't believe it," Bess whispered. "Justin?"

"He's obsessed with you, Bess. And you've got to talk to him before he hurts somebody," Nancy said.

"Obsessed with me?" Bess felt as if she had just woken from a dream only to be plunked down in a nightmare. Justin was going to set off a bomb and kill people because of her!

Chapter 13

Montana looked across the studio at Cory. She'd give anything to be able to hold his hand right then, but Justin wouldn't let them sit near each other. If either one of them tried anything, Justin would set off the bomb—of that, Montana was sure.

She didn't know how much more she could take. She had already bitten all her fingernails down to the quick. Her stomach was in knots. She had never been more scared in her life.

After Montana had turned over the station's microphone to Justin, he'd introduced himself to the radio audience and started talking about how much he loved Bess. He described how he'd set off the bomb at the theater so that he could save her. He wanted to do so much for her. His wild ranting made no sense to Montana. Whenever she or Cory tried to talk to him, he threatened to blow the place up. Her only hope was that somebody out there was actually tuned in to her show and would alert the police.

At first Montana had worried that Ray would appear late for the interview, startle Justin, and they'd all be killed. But apparently he'd never had any intention of showing up. Montana couldn't care less, at the moment. She never wanted to do another radio interview—even if she got the chance. If she lived past today.

"Bess, if you're out there," Justin spoke into the microphone, "listen to me. You've got to listen. You've got to believe me. And believe in me. I know you don't know me that well. And maybe you have a hard time trusting people. But you can trust me, Bess."

Trust him to kill you! Montana thought, growing more and more annoyed by Justin's monologue.

"I'd never hurt you, Bess. I love you. I don't know why you can't see that. But once you and I are together—"

"Attention, please! Attention!" A megaphone blared outside. "This is the police!"

Finally! Montana thought. She cast a look in Cory's direction, and he smiled back at her.

Justin leaped out of his chair and rushed to the window, lifting two slats of the venetian blinds so he could peek out. "Go away!" he shouted.

"This is Sergeant Gianelli. Justin, we know

you're in there. Come out with your hands up," the megaphone boomed.

"No!" Justin shouted. He rushed back to the microphone. "Bess, don't listen to them. Don't let them stop you from coming here, to me. I won't hurt you—I couldn't hurt you."

"Justin, if you won't come out, at least let your hostages go," the sergeant said.

"They're not going anywhere until I know Bess has heard me," Justin said over the air.

There was silence outside. Then suddenly the telephone inside the studio rang. Montana jumped at the noise—her first sensation was that the bomb had gone off.

"Answer it," Justin commanded.

"But you said not to move," Montana protested.

"I said answer it!" Justin cried.

Montana grabbed the telephone. "H-hello?"

"This is Sergeant Gianelli. Is this Montana?" a voice asked.

"Yes," Montana said nervously.

"Is it Bess?" Justin asked eagerly.

"No, Justin. It's not Bess," Montana said.

"Then hang up!" he commanded. "She might be trying to get through."

"I—I have to go," Montana told the police sergeant.

"Stay on the line!" he commanded. "Are you okay? Don't hang up."

"Get rid of them," Justin told her. "Bess, if you're trying to call, and you get a busy signal, try back. I'm waiting here for you. Get off the phone, Montana!" he screamed. *"Now!"*

Montana dropped the receiver into the cradle, her hand shaking.

"Quit calling us. Stop bothering me! I have a lot of things to take care of. I have to concentrate." Justin spoke into the microphone in a strained voice. "Everyone just back off, right now, or I'll blow this place sky-high. I did it before. Don't think I won't do it again."

"Justin, calm down," Cory said in a soothing voice. "It'll be okay. Bess is coming. I'm sure of it."

Justin turned from the microphone. "How do you know?"

"Justin, she cares about you. She'll be here," Cory said.

Montana looked at him. It might not work, but Cory had just bought them a little more time. Come on, Bess. Come on, police, she thought desperately. Somebody, anybody . . . I don't want to die in here!

"She's taking a big risk, but we'll be right behind her with backup," Sergeant Gianelli told Nancy, Michael, and Max.

"Are you sure she should go in there?" Max asked.

"Sorry, Max, but our best hope that Justin will surrender is if Bess talks to him," Nancy said. She gazed up at the studio windows. The blinds were still closed. "Bess, are you still willing to do this?"

"Yes," Bess said. "I don't want anybody to get hurt."

"Here's what we'll do," Sergeant Gianelli said. "Bess, you'll go in first. We'll cover you. As soon as you can get Justin away from the bomb, our guys can get in there and grab him. We get the bomb out of there, and everyone's okay. The hostages *and* you. All set? I don't want to wait any longer."

"I'm ready," Bess said. Max squeezed her hand in a show of support.

"So am I," Michael said. "This is going to make awesome footage."

"Oh, no. You two don't go in until we give the okay," Sergeant Gianelli told Michael. "I don't want anything compromising Bess or the hostages."

"But it's an incredible story," Michael protested.

"And you'll be here to cover it when Justin comes *out* of that building," his father said. "Not before."

Michael tried negotiating. "Dad, if it weren't for us, you wouldn't have Bess to talk to Justin, and the situation would be even worse. Cut us some slack, huh? Let us in the building?"

"I don't have time for this. I'm coordinating a hostage rescue," his father said tersely. *"Stay out!"*

Bess slowly walked toward the radio station building, flanked by police officers.

"Bess is on her way," Sergeant Gianelli yelled through the megaphone. "Justin, when there's a knock at the door, answer it. It's Bess. She needs to talk to you."

"Come on, let's go," Michael said, once the group had gone into the building. "We'll just get within sound and visual range so we can film it."

"But—" began Nancy.

"Are you coming?" Michael asked. He didn't wait for an answer but took off for the entrance.

"Of course," said Nancy, who hadn't waited to answer before taking off.

As they tiptoed into the second-floor hallway, well behind the police, Nancy heard the studio door open. "Justin?" Bess said in a timid voice. "Justin, I got your messages. What's wrong?"

"What took you so long?" Justin said angrily.

"I'm sorry. I didn't have the radio on," Bess said. "I didn't know—"

"How could you not know? I've been so obvious. I *told* you how I felt about you—"

"No, you didn't," Bess said.

"Yes, I did!" Justin yelled. "You weren't paying attention! You never do! But you'll have to pay attention when I blow this place up—"

"Justin, please! *Please* don't do that," Bess begged. "I'm here now. I'm paying attention."

Nancy paced back and forth. She couldn't take much more of this. She felt like rushing in and knocking Justin to the ground herself.

"I honestly didn't realize the depth of your feelings," Bess continued. "But that's my fault. And I'm sorry, Justin."

"When I set off that bomb next to you and saved you? Didn't you know how I felt about you then?"

Justin demanded. Nancy heard him start to cry. "I'd do anything for you, Bess. Anything."

"Maybe you could hug me, then," Bess said. "Because I never meant to hurt you, Justin."

There was the sound of a chair clattering to the floor and then Bess's soothing voice. "I'm sorry, Justin. I'm so sorry," she said.

The six police officers in the hall burst into the studio. Michael ran forward with his camera, capturing it all on film. Montana and Cory ran out of the room, holding on to each other. Two of the officers quickly led them past Nancy and down the stairwell.

"On the floor! Arms and legs spread!" an officer ordered Justin.

Two more police officers, from the bomb squad, ran into the studio and studied the bomb. "It's okay," an officer announced. "This can only be set off by a flame."

Nancy heaved a sigh of relief. They were all going to make it out alive.

"You have the right to remain silent," another officer began as he took Justin down the hall in handcuffs. Justin raised his head as he passed Nancy.

"I love you, Bess!" he cried. "Never forget!"

An officer led Bess down the hall and left her with Nancy. Bess looked at her friend, with tears streaming down her face. "I feel so awful!"

Nancy put her arms around Bess and hugged her tightly. "It's not your fault, Bess," she said compassionately. "This shouldn't have happened to you. It had nothing to do with you, only Justin."

"But Justin—he'll go to jail," Bess said. "And he's . . ."

"He needs help, Bess. He'll go to a hospital," Nancy said. "Remember, he didn't hurt anybody."

"No. But he tried," Bess said, stepping away and gazing back at the studio. "Imagine if he killed Montana and Cory . . . for my sake."

"But he didn't," Nancy said, "and everything's going to be okay now."

Nancy looked around for Michael. When she saw him, he was up against the wall with his father's finger pointed at his chest. "Michael, do you or do you not know the meaning of 'stay out'?" Sergeant Gianelli demanded.

"Come on, Bess," Nancy said. "Let's get out of here."

As they walked out of the building, Max rushed up to Bess. Brian and George were right behind him. "Bess! Are you okay?" George asked.

Bess nodded, giving her cousin a hug. "I think so."

"I was so worried when I heard Justin on the radio," Brian said. "By the time I got here, you were inside." He brushed the tears off Bess's cheeks first, and then his own.

"It was pretty scary," Bess admitted. "I don't know whether to laugh or to cry."

"Me, too." Max took Bess's hand.

"Me three," Nancy said, hugging Bess again.

"Me four," George cheered, putting her arms around Nancy and Bess.

"Hey," Brian said. "Me five!" And he hugged them all at once.

"Do you want to get a soda or coffee or something?" Cory asked Montana. They'd just finished giving their statements to the police. "Or go for a walk? I don't think I can go back to my dorm room right now."

"Me neither," Montana said. "I'm still really freaked out." She tried to sling her backpack over her shoulder, but she couldn't seem to hold on to it. It fell to the ground.

"We're okay." Cory put his hands around hers. "You were really brave."

"No, I wasn't." Montana looked down at the dropped backpack, embarrassed. "I completely folded."

"You did not," Cory said. "You did what Justin asked. You didn't crack under the strain. If you had, or I had—"

"We'd be toast now," Montana said, biting her lip.

"Montana, look. There's something I've been meaning to say to you for a while. Now that we almost lost our lives together, I want to get it out," Cory said.

"Let's go on that walk you suggested," Montana hastily said. She picked up her backpack and turned in the direction of the lake. The temperature was freezing, but Montana felt flushed.

They walked in silence, until Montana couldn't stand it any longer. It was time to face up to what had happened that night at Club Z.

"So," she began. "You were about to say that you overheard me ask Ray out—bare my soul—only to be shot down. Believe me, I remember you were there. You were the sole witness to my humiliation and demise." She pointed to a large bank of snow at the lake's edge. "Shall we bury me there? You can plant flowers over my grave in the spring. That would be romantic, wouldn't it?"

"Why would I want to bury you?" Cory asked in astonishment.

"You can't possibly let me live after discovering what a loser I am. Just be quick about it. I hate reruns of humiliation."

Cory laughed. "You have many talents, Montana, but I didn't know you had such a flair for melodrama."

"I am rising to the occasion, Cory." Montana smiled sadly. She paused and her mind returned to *that* night. "It was so embarrassing! And worse, someone—you—were there. You and Ray probably had a pretty good laugh back at the loft over pathetic Montana Smith." She waited for a response. Cory said nothing.

"I can't stand this!" Montana turned as if to run, but Cory reached out and caught the sleeve of her leather jacket.

Cory noticed that a few tears had begun to run down Montana's cheeks.

"First," he said authoritatively, "forget about

Ray. *That's* what I've been wanting to tell you, Montana. Ray's just a joe like anybody else. I know for a fact that he's no knight in shining armor. Remember, we're in the same band. I know him pretty well."

Montana brushed a tear from her face. "Are you always so loyal to your friends? I wonder what Ray says about you behind your back."

"The same thing! Because it's true. Girls are always looking for some Mr. Perfect Guy, but, you know, we're all just guys. Now, can we forget about Ray?"

"I don't know if I'll ever live down being brushed off—" Montana began to whine.

"Forget Ray!" Cory cried out loudly, which jolted Montana. "Montana, you're so beautiful. You're smart and creative. You could have any guy on campus."

"Except Ray," muttered Montana.

Cory took a step backward and was about to walk away when Montana shouted, "Forget Ray!" She sidled up to Cory and looked him straight in the eye. "You really think I could get any man on campus?"

"Any," Cory confirmed.

"Even you?"

"I didn't mean to say . . ." Cory turned red and stared at his shoes like a little boy. "I didn't mean me."

"Why not?" Montana asked. "If I can have any guy on campus, maybe the guy I really want is you."

"Do you mean that, Montana?" Cory asked. Montana nodded. In the silence they kissed.

"You know," Cory began after they had reluctantly parted. "I was hoping to get the chance to kiss you someday." He held her close. "What do I mean, hoping? More like praying. On a daily basis."

"Come on, you haven't liked me for *that* long," Montana said. "You just fell for your cohostage."

"No." Cory shook his head. "I've been wanting to ask you out for weeks now, but you didn't have eyes for anyone but Ray—"

"Ray?" Montana asked innocently. "Ray who? Oh, him! Forget about him. He's history." She leaned in and kissed Cory again. "And I mean that."

"I don't know if you do," Cory said with a smile. "Try to convince me."

Montana pressed herself against Cory and kissed him until he was certain.

CHAPTER 14

"Here it comes . . . three, two, one . . . action!" Kara cried. Suite 301 was full of Nancy's friends. The television was on. It had been two weeks since the pipe bomb explosion at Hewlitt.

"This is so exciting!" Reva said.

"Nancy Drew's career, part one, her television debut," Ginny said in a serious voice, as if she were narrating a filmstrip.

"You guys! Don't put *too* much pressure on her or anything," Bess joked.

Nancy leaned forward on the couch. She'd seen videotape of herself before, but she'd never actually watched herself on TV. With all of her friends peering over her shoulder at the same time, she couldn't help but feel nervous. What if she looked foolish, or sounded as if she didn't know what she was doing? What if . . . ?

At least the story about Justin was strong. She knew that. Even if *she* didn't hold up, the material would.

"Nancy, you look awesome," Eileen commented.

"Especially considering that the camera adds ten pounds," Casey said.

"Did you happen to mention on camera that you live in Thayer three-oh-one, and that you have an incredibly cute, single suitemate?" Ginny asked.

"Shh! The report's starting," Reva said as the opening credits and show jingle ended.

"Good evening, and welcome to *Headlines,*" Nancy said. "I'm Nancy Drew."

"And I'm Michael Gianelli. Our top story this week? 'Love Gone Awry.'"

The live audience in 301 booed and hissed.

"He made up that title—I didn't," Nancy told them.

"It began innocently enough, with a school play. And it ended, almost tragically, in a hostage situation. Now, with exclusive footage, we bring you the story of Justin Beckett, a student who wanted to put the woman he loved in danger, so that he could come to her rescue."

Nancy watched as a psychiatrist discussed Justin's problem, and as Sergeant Gianelli explained how Justin had stolen the firecrackers from the Beta house. Apparently, Justin had gotten the idea of making a bomb from recent news coverage of a similar bombing.

Reva let out a breath when the report was over. "Bess, I'm so sorry about what happened."

"He sounds really disturbed," Kara said.

"But he'll probably benefit a lot from the counseling he's getting," Nancy said.

."I hope so," Bess said. "This is going to sound crazy, but despite everything, I think that deep down he meant well. He really did. It's hard for me to imagine his hurting anyone."

"He could have, though," Reva said critically. "What if somebody had picked up that first pipe bomb?"

"Or what if he had set off the bomb at the radio station?" George asked.

"You're right, you're all right. But I can't ignore my feelings—any of them. Believe me, I'm more than glad that Nancy pursued the story, or we might not have caught him in time," Bess said.

"Don't thank just me," Nancy said. "Thank Michael, too. He actually did help." She shrugged. "Go figure."

Sergeant Lawrence Gianelli sat grinning ear to ear as he watched the closing credits for *Headlines* scroll down the television screen. Reporter, cohost, and coproducer: Michael Gianelli.

"So, what did you think, Dad?" Michael asked from his front-row seat on the floor. His father sat at one end of the couch behind him and his buddy Gus sat at the other.

"I know it's corny, Michael," Mr. Gianelli said

softly, "but it's at times like this I wish your mother were still with us. She would have been so proud."

Michael smiled at his father. "Can I take that to mean that *you* are proud?"

His father laughed. "All that education you've been getting seems to have made you quite a psychologist."

Now it was Gus's turn to laugh, a little too loudly and a little too long. "Sarge, I'm sorry." He panted and laughed between words. "Really. It's just that your son here can also be so stupid."

"Well, *I* know that. I am his father. But, just how do *you* know?" Mr. Gianelli asked.

Michael stood up, interrupting the conversation. "Gus, don't you have to go and study for one of the courses you're failing?"

"Ha, ha, very funny," he retorted. "Your father has asked me a question, and I think he should get an answer." Gus smiled mischievously.

Gus saw by the look on his friend's face that he didn't think this was funny.

"Look, Mike, I'm kidding. What's with you, man?" Gus asked.

Michael's face relaxed slightly. "Okay, I'm just a little tense—okay?—watching my first performance cohosting a news show. Okay?"

"Mike," said his father. "Chill out. Have a seat here."

"Hey, dude," Gus said, slapping Michael's back as he sat on the couch. "The show was great. You were great. The only complaint I got is the name—what was it called?"

"Yeah," Michael agreed with a huff. " 'Love Gone Awry.' That was Nancy's idea."

"I thought it was a fine title," Mr. Gianelli said. "And I thought Nancy did a wonderful job, too. You work well together, and she sure is a looker—"

"Dad!"

"Precisely my point of view, Mr. G., but he won't listen to me. They had this challenge to set each other up with the perfect date, and what does he do? He sets *me* up with Lois Lane—"

"Nancy," Michael translated for his father.

"Now, what we were supposed to have in common, I don't know. She's all smart, talented, and beautiful."

"Now, Gus, don't sell yourself short," said the voice of age and experience.

"No, Mr. G.," Gus protested. "I'm cool, but why me? Where are *his* brain cells?" Gus slapped Michael on the top of his head. "Wouldn't it have been smarter to show up himself as her date?"

Mr. Gianelli rubbed his chin. "Hmm, I see what you mean, Gus. Makes me wonder where I went wrong. Wasn't I a good father? I taught him everything I knew about the birds and the bees, but it doesn't seem to have sunk in." Gus and Mr. Gianelli could hardly keep from laughing.

"Hey, you two," Michael barked, "lay off. I agree, she's beautiful, she's smart, and, yes, she's almost as talented as I am. But aren't you going to listen to my side?"

"So, what does the defendant have to say for himself?" Mr. Gianelli asked.

"That Nancy Drew is impossible. Whenever I try to scoop her, she's always on the scene. She cuts down every idea of mine and bad-mouths me to our sponsor, Stanley Trenton."

"Yo," Gus interrupted. "I think you've got that one twisted around. I was there when you called Trenton and tried to get Nancy bumped off the bomb story. She had every right to give you a piece of her mind."

Michael gave Gus a look that meant if he opened his mouth once more, he'd lose some teeth.

"She just can't sit back and let me do the work," Michael finished up.

"Well, son," Mr. Gianelli said, "I don't think that's her job. In fact, it sounds like the fact that she is doing her job and doing it well has gotten under your skin."

There was silence between the three men. A loud advertisement for a local amusement park blared from the television. "Ride the wild tornado!" the announcer cried. Michael picked up the remote and silenced him.

"That's what she is, Dad, a wild tornado."

"But you like challenges," prodded his father.

Michael was cornered.

"I give," he said. "You want the truth? Nancy Drew is hot: beautiful, talented, smart. We all agree. But there is something more to her, some spark, some spark of fire that lands on me whenever we're working together. Whether we're fighting or—it happens sometimes—agreeing, that spark leaps out and burns me."

"Uh-oh," Gus moaned.

"It's that bad?" Michael's father asked.

Michael put his head in his hands. "It's that bad and it's that good."

"Nancy was a total natural," Bess commented as she and George walked back to Jamison Hall after watching *Headlines*. Bess pulled her scarf more tightly around her neck.

"Are you surprised?" George asked. "I'm not." She shivered. "She already knows how to write great stories, and she's completely comfortable in front of the camera."

"I wish I felt that comfortable," Bess confessed.

"Bess, are you kidding me? You love being the center of attention. You're the most natural born actor of any of us," George teased.

"I might *look* natural, but I get incredibly nervous. Being the center of attention isn't always a good thing," Bess said.

"No. Especially not when there's some psycho around trying to hurt you," George said. "I know you feel sorry for Justin, but I can't. If he'd done anything to hurt you, Bess . . ."

"Don't think about it," Bess said. Once again she thought of what Daphne had said. All in all, it was good advice. "In the words of the immortal Daphne, 'Get over it already. You're all right, aren't you?'" George's mouth dropped open, and they both started laughing.

Bess pulled her scarf up over her mouth and nose. "What is it, ten degrees or something?"

"Something like that. And I have a feeling it's just about to get colder." George gestured to the figure approaching them. "Here comes the immortal Daphne, herself."

"We'd better run for cover," Bess cautioned. "Oops, too late."

"Bess. You shouldn't be out in the cold. You might ruin your voice," Daphne said.

"Hi, Daphne," Bess said. "I'm surprised you're not worried about the same thing. When you finally get me out of the way, you want to be ready for the play, don't you?"

Daphne glared at her. "I never tried to get you out of the way. But I can understand you're disappointed that I wasn't the bomber. After all, that would have made everything so much easier for you. I'd have gone off to jail, and you wouldn't have had to compete with me for the next production. But I'm still around, Bess. And next time, I expect you to be *my* understudy."

"Don't hold your breath," George told her. "Bess will be auditioning for the lead in the next show, too."

"Exactly my point," Daphne said in a superior tone. She continued walking as if she'd never even lowered herself to stop and chat with the peasants.

"I have only one thing to say about her," Bess told George, watching Daphne walk into Thayer. "And that's . . . What*ever!*"

"I'm going to miss you." Jonathan stopped the car in the parking lot outside Thayer Hall. He was dropping Stephanie off on his way out of town, bound for a week-long work seminar in Chicago.

True to form, Stephanie had convinced him that while he was gone, she should stay in her old suite on campus. Casey hadn't gotten another roommate yet, and he wouldn't have to worry about her being alone. She didn't mention to him that she was really looking forward to partying all night long, every night.

"I'll miss you, too, honey," Stephanie told him. She *would* miss Jonathan. She realized suddenly that she really had gotten used to living with him. On the other hand, it would be nice to hang out with her friends. Stephanie could use a major dose of freedom right about now. She finally understood those old song lyrics about not knowing what you've got until it's gone.

"Attention," the car radio crackled, "the winter storm watch for the Weston area has just been upgraded to a winter storm warning. The storm is moving eastward and has dumped over a foot of snow on parts of Nebraska and Iowa. The storm should hit Weston early tomorrow morning. Stay posted for further bulletins."

"Wow. You're getting out just in time," Stephanie commented.

"And you're getting settled *in* just in time," Jonathan told her.

"Will you make it to Chicago before the storm hits?" Stephanie asked.

"Sure, don't worry. Since the drive's only a few

hours and I'm going east, I should stay ahead of it," Jonathan said.

"Then you'd better take off right now," Stephanie said, concerned.

"It's okay, Steph. *Don't worry,*" Jonathan told her again.

"But I am worried." Stephanie threw open the passenger door and walked to the trunk, to get out her gym bag. As she struggled to pick it up, she wondered why she'd packed so much—she was only staying at Thayer for a week. Of course, there would be all those parties and she'd need a change of clothes for each one. Not to mention the clothes she needed for everything else: all—well, most—of the unmarried-type things she didn't get to do anymore.

She hurried around to Jonathan's side of the car. "Okay, have fun at the seminar," she said. "I'll see you next week."

"Not so fast!" Jonathan laughed as he opened the door, stepping out of the car. "I'm in a hurry, but I still have time to kiss my wife goodbye." He wrapped his arms around Stephanie's waist and pulled her toward him. "I can't imagine not seeing you for a whole week. It's going to be horrible. You take care of yourself. I'll call you every night."

"Okay." Stephanie kissed him goodbye. "Now get going—it's freezing out here!"

"You're such a romantic." Jonathan smiled, kissed her again, then climbed back into the car.

Stephanie waved at him until he pulled out of

the parking lot. Then she turned around, picked up her bag, and ran into the dorm.

The door to Suite 301 was open, and the lounge was filled with people.

"What are you guys doing?" Stephanie asked, pausing in the doorway. "You didn't tell me there was a party tonight."

"We were just watching Nancy's new TV show," Kara said. "Did you catch it?"

"No, sorry," Stephanie said to Nancy. She dumped her gym bag in the middle of the floor. "Jonathan was working late at the store, and I was waiting to get a ride over here."

"So he left for Chicago?" Casey asked.

"Yes. Good thing, too, because a huge snowstorm is coming tomorrow." Stephanie found an empty space on the couch and snuggled into it. She couldn't believe how good it felt to be back. Now it was time to have some fun. "So, who wants to go out tonight?" she asked.

"Stephanie, didn't you just say that a major winter storm is headed this way?" Casey replied.

"What's your point?" Stephanie asked.

"We might want to stay in tonight," Casey said. "Order a pizza, watch a couple of movies . . ."

"Come on, that's so boring," Stephanie protested. "Haven't you guys ever been out during a winter storm? It's so much fun! You get trapped wherever you are and then you have to spend the night—"

"What exactly are you proposing?" Casey asked, raising her eyebrows. "I thought you were happily married."

"Oh, I am. But I could stand a little fun for a change," Stephanie said.

"For a change?" Nancy asked.

Embarrassed at what she'd let slip, Stephanie tried to laugh it off. "Oh, you know what I mean!"

"Does Jonathan know the only reason you wanted to stay on campus was for the parties?" Kara teased.

"Jonathan trusts me," Stephanie declared. Probably more than he should, she thought, and definitely more than I trust myself. "Anyway, do you think he'll hole up in his hotel room with so many great clubs to go to? Give me a break. In any case, I'm certainly not going to stay in just because he's not here. Don't you think you guys are being a little old-fashioned?"

"I think that if it's ten degrees and snowing, I'd rather be snuggled up in bed than dancing at Club Z and wondering how I'm going to make it home," Kara said.

"Then I'll have to go by myself," Stephanie said with a shrug. Fine. She met more people when she went out alone, anyway. She'd have a great time.

"Take a sled," Casey said. "You never know when you might need one."

Everyone started laughing. Stephanie frowned. "Remind me again why I wanted to spend a week in this suite?"

"It's the love, babe," Kara said, wrapping her arm around Stephanie's neck and squeezing her tightly.

"The friendship," Casey said, squishing her on the other side.

"The crazy people," Stephanie said, smiling despite herself. "Now quit choking me!"

"I can't believe the play's been over for a week," Max said as he and Bess stood in line at Java Joe's on Saturday morning.

"Neither can I," Bess said. "We do all that work, and then we have four performances."

"It's not Broadway," Max said.

"It isn't?" Bess looked up at him. "Then what was I doing wasting my time with it?"

Max grinned. "You decided to share your talent with the little people of Weston, remember?"

"Yes. That's it," Bess said, nodding.

"May I help you?" the clerk asked as Bess and Max moved to the front of the line.

"Tea with lemon, please," Bess said. She glanced at the refrigerator case full of pastries: cherry pie, cheesecake, oatmeal raisin cookies . . . Everything looked delicious.

"Would you like anything else?" the woman behind the counter asked.

"No, thanks," she replied without a thought. Bess shook her head in surprise. The decision had come naturally to her. She turned to Max. "Do you want anything?"

"Just a coffee. And you," he said.

Bess laughed. "And I thought *I* was a mushy romantic."

"Pushy, maybe. Mushy, no," Max teased as he

took his mug of coffee from the clerk and handed her money for both of their beverages.

Bess pinched his arm. "I'm not pushy!"

"Oh, I guess that would be me, then," Max said with a smile. "Come on, let's get a table."

Bess picked up her mug of hot tea in one hand and held Max's hand with the other. Maybe the pieces were falling into place, like George had said. For good, Bess thought, smiling at Max as they sat close together. Or even better, just for right now.

Here I am, Bess thought, maybe for the first time ever, just happy in this moment. Vicky's always telling me in therapy: live in the moment! I'm not obsessing about Paul and I'm not obsessing about food.

She raised her mug and looked fondly at Max. "Here's to tomorrow," she said.

NEXT IN NANCY DREW ON CAMPUS™:

Getting snowed in can be exciting, unpredictable, and a little dangerous. And at Wilder, the fun and games are just beginning. . . . Ray broke up with Ginny and pushed Montana away. Now he's having second thoughts—about both. But he may not get a second chance with either. He may just end up out in the cold. Nancy's out in the cold, too—except she's got company: her costar and rival, Michael. Investigating an investment scheme that may be a scam, they get a hot lead that takes them off campus and directly into the path of the blizzard. And when the storm hits, they may make some surprising discoveries . . . about each other . . . in *Snowbound,* Nancy Drew on Campus #25.